October's menu
BARONESSA GELATERIA
in Boston's North End

In addition to our regular flavors of
gelato, this month we are featuring:

• Angel food cake with fresh whipped cream

At seventeen, small-town girl Celia had never
been out of her home state, never let loose,
never been kissed. But when Reese Baronè
spent a summer at the Cape, a lot changed.
His sexy swagger stirred her senses and made
her lose control.

• Dark, rich devil's food cake

Reese was privileged, monied; he knew what he
wanted and usually got it. And he wanted Celia.
One touch and she was his. He knew she could
never resist him—and after he fled, he knew he
could never forget her....

• Hot fudge sundae

Their lovemaking thirteen years ago was
child's play compared to the heat that flared
between them at Reese's return. No longer a
sweet innocent, Celia was a woman now, with
a woman's needs. As much as she wanted to
deny them, her body betrayed her with an all-
out yearning for Reese's expert hands and
sensuous mouth. She'd spent most of her life
trying to forget them.... Now she wanted to
revel in them—rumors be damned—for as
long as it lasted....

Bud

Dear Reader,

Thanks for choosing Silhouette Desire, *the* place to find passionate, powerful and provocative love stories. We're starting off the month in style with Diana Palmer's *Man in Control*, a LONG, TALL TEXANS story and the author's 100th book! Congratulations, Diana, and thank you so much for each and every one of your wonderful stories.

Our continuing series DYNASTIES: THE BARONES is back this month with Anne Marie Winston's thrilling tale *Born To Be Wild*. And Cindy Gerard gives us a fabulous story about a woman who finds romance at her best friend's wedding, in *Tempting the Tycoon*. Weddings seem to be the place to meet a romantic partner (note to self: get invited to more weddings), as we find in Shawna Delacorte's *Having the Best Man's Baby*.

Also this month, Kathie DeNosky is back with another title in her ongoing ranching series—don't miss *Lonetree Ranchers: Morgan* and watch for the final story in this trilogy coming in December. Finally, welcome back the wonderful Emilie Rose with *Cowboy's Million-Dollar Secret*, a fantastic story about a man who inherits much more than he ever expected.

More passion to you!

Melissa Jeglinski

Melissa Jeglinski
Senior Editor
Silhouette Desire

Please address questions and book requests to:
Silhouette Reader Service
U.S.: 3010 Walden Ave., P.O. Box 1325, Buffalo, NY 14269
Canadian: P.O. Box 609, Fort Erie, Ont. L2A 5X3

Born To Be Wild

ANNE MARIE WINSTON

Silhouette® Desire

Published by Silhouette Books

America's Publisher of Contemporary Romance

Special thanks and acknowledgment are given to Anne Marie Winston for her contribution to the DYNASTIES: THE BARONES series.

To Kathleenest
The bestest roommate ever.

SILHOUETTE BOOKS

ISBN 0-373-76538-X

BORN TO BE WILD

Visit Silhouette at www.eHarlequin.com

Printed in U.S.A.

ANNE MARIE WINSTON

RITA® Award finalist and bestselling author Anne Marie Winston loves babies she can give back when they cry, animals in all shapes and sizes and just about anything that blooms. When she's not writing, she's managing a house full of animals and teenagers, reading anything she can find and trying *not* to eat chocolate. She will dance at the slightest provocation and weeds her gardens when she can't see the sun for the weeds anymore. You can learn more about Anne Marie's novels by visiting her Web site at www.annemariewinston.com.

DYNASTIES:
THE
BARONES

Meet the Barones of Boston—
an elite clan caught in a web of danger,
deceit…and desire!

Who's Who in
BORN TO BE WILD

Reese Barone—He's made a killing in the stock market
and has seen picturesque sunsets all around the world,
but he finally realizes that when he walked away thirteen
years ago, he lost everything that mattered. Family…and
Celia, the only woman he's ever loved….

Celia Papaleo—Something strange is happening at her
harbor in Cape Cod. Something she suspects is linked
to the mysterious deaths of her husband and young son.
Even stranger is the return of her one—and only—true
love, Reese. His return is the one thing she dreaded—
and the one thing she craved….

Nicholas Barone—He knows all about reunions. Some
fail miserably…and some are worth waiting for. Which
will his brother's be?

Prologue

"**S**he said *what?*" Twenty-one-year-old Reese Barone, seated in the parlor of his family home in Boston's Beacon Hill district, stared at his father in shock. "She's lying!"

"Eliza Mayhew says that she's pregnant and you are the father." Carlo Barone stood in front of the elaborate marble fireplace, hands clasped behind his back. He eyed his second-to-eldest son sternly. "Needless to say, your mother and I are very disappointed in you, Reese. Let's not make this more difficult than it already is."

"But I never—"

"Reese." His father's voice was colder than he'd ever heard it, even more so than the time Reese had been caught and disciplined for putting two baby goats in the headmaster's office on April Fools' Day. The fact that he hadn't taken into account their tendency to eat everything in sight—and promptly re-cycle it from the other end—had been a significant problem. "There will be no discussion. You will do the right thing and marry Miss Mayhew at the end of the month."

"I—huh? I will not." Reese leaped to his feet, nearly upsetting the elegant wing chair in which he'd been sitting while he'd waited to find out what could possibly have gotten his old man's drawers in such a twist. "That baby isn't mine."

On the love seat facing them, his mother, Moira, bowed her head as a sob escaped.

Carlo's face darkened with anger. "Haven't you already done enough to damage our family name?" he demanded. "First you get involved with that fish-erman's daughter in Harwichport—"

"There's nothing wrong with Celia," Reese said hotly, "except that she doesn't come with a pedi-gree."

"It's not the lack of family connections," his mother said. "I would hope you know us better than that. It's just that… Oh, Reese, she's so young. And she comes from a world that's very different from yours—"

"Being of Portuguese descent doesn't make her different."

But his mother ignored the rebuke. "How could you ever expect to have anything in common?"

"Besides the obvious," put in his father. "Which, might I point out, you appear to have in common with other women, as well."

"I already told you," Reese said tightly, "I can't be the father of Eliza's baby. I—"

"Enough!" Carlo made an angry gesture. "I will

not tolerate lying. Miss Mayhew is the daughter of a family friend as well as a classmate of your sister's. How could you be so careless?''

''Has she had a paternity test done?'' Reese demanded. ''Maybe you'd better think about who's being careless.'' He could feel his temper slipping the tight leash he'd held, and the words spilled out. Even the pain in his father's eyes couldn't halt his tongue. ''Taking someone else's word without giving me a chance to defend myself? Fine.'' His eyes narrowed. ''I don't need this, Dad. I'm not marrying Lying Eliza and you can't make me.'' He strode toward the door to the hallway.

''Don't you dare walk away when I'm speaking to you!'' Reese had come by his temper honestly. Carlo stepped forward and reached for his son's arm, but Reese shoved him away in a red haze of anger.

''You ever put your hands on me again and I swear you'll be sorry,'' he snarled at his father. He barreled down the hall to the heavy front door, oblivious to his mother's frantic cries. As he slammed through the door and the thunderous sound of its closing echoed behind him, he swore one thing to himself: he would never set foot in the same room with his father again until he'd received an apology from the old man.

His chest was tight with pain and he blinked rapidly. No way, he told himself, *no way* was he ever going into that house again until his father apologized. He couldn't be the father of that baby—he'd never even slept with Eliza! But he hadn't been allowed the chance to explain. Hell, his father hadn't even given him the courtesy of pretending he might be innocent.

He was getting as fast and far away from Massachusetts as he could on the first flight out. To hell with finishing school. Who needed a degree from Harvard, anyway? He was good with the stock market, had already managed to significantly increase the million he'd inherited on his last birthday.

But...if he quit school, what would he do?

The answer came to him as easily as if the idea had only been waiting for the question to be asked. He'd dreamed of sailing around the world since he'd been old enough to steer a boat.

Around the world! Oh, yeah, he was outta here.

As he jumped into his car and roared away from his childhood home for the last time, he decided he'd ask Celia daSilva to join him. Images of her naked body glowing in the golden sunlight filled his head. God, he loved her. They could even get married!

Then cold sanity kicked in. Celia wouldn't be eighteen for over another month. Wouldn't his father just love the chance to catch him with a minor! And he knew Celia's father wasn't exactly thrilled that she had been glued to Reese's side all summer.

Five more weeks...

He couldn't stick around that long. Anger continued to race through him. He could barely wait to get out of town. Today. Besides, he knew Celia too well. If he went to her now, she would try to talk him into waiting until he was calmer, into talking with his father. And if that failed, she'd pester him to take her along. The hell of it was, he wasn't sure he had the willpower to resist her. Even if it landed him in jail if they were caught.

He'd write to her. Write her and tell her what his father had done, explain to her why he'd had to leave so abruptly. She would understand. That was the one thing he could count on. Celia always understood him. Yeah, he'd write. Ask her to come with him after her birthday…ask her to marry him.

His hands tightened on the wheel as he punched the accelerator of his sleek sports car against the floorboard. To hell with his old man. He didn't need anyone else as long as he had Celia.

One

"Hey, Celia! Guess what I heard?"

With an abstracted smile Celia Papaleo glanced up from the paperwork on permanent moorings. Thank God it was finally October. They'd reached that time of year when Harwichport residents could begin to breathe again after the tourists overran Cape Cod for the summer, flinging money and flouting rules and generally making the South Harwich harbormaster and everyone else who worked for her crazy.

"Roma." She raised her head and smiled at the petite woman in the bright red sweater who'd entered her office, sitting back in her chair. "What did you hear?"

Roma had been Celia's best friend since their elementary school days. She held a tiny girl in one arm and a toddler by the hand.

Celia rose and automatically reached for the infant, ignoring the sharp sting of pain that pierced her heart as she cuddled baby Irene close. How she'd loved holding Leo this way when he was a baby. Leo... He would have been five next week—

"Ceel?" Roma snapped her fingers, waving one hand in front of Celia's face.

Celia focused on her friend's concerned blue eyes, knowing Roma would worry. Pushing aside the grief that inevitably welled up, she made an effort to smile again.

"Sorry," she said. "I was just thinking how glad I am summer's over."

"Amen to that." Roma's voice held feeling although she still studied Celia too closely. "Adios, tourists."

"Those tourists put food on our tables," Celia felt compelled to point out.

"Yeah, but they're still a huge pain in the—"

"All right. I get your point." Celia chuckled. She gestured to Irene and little William, who was busy pushing a truck around the seat of one office chair with pudgy fingers. "So what's so important that you had to drag these two down here instead of just picking up the phone?"

"Oh!" Roma perked up. "Almost forgot. You'd better sit down," she warned darkly.

Celia's eyebrows rose. "Why?"

"Reese Barone docked over at Saquatucket Marina last night."

Reese Barone...Reese Barone...Reese Barone... The name echoed through her head, a blast from the past she surely could have lived the rest of her life without hearing. Her muscles tensed, her heart skipped a beat. For a single crystalline instant, the world froze. Then she forced herself to react.

"Wow." Her voice would be calm if it killed her. "It's been years since he was here, hasn't it?"

Roma snorted. "You know darn well how long it's been. He hasn't been back since he dumped you for the pregnant deb."

"Technically, he didn't dump me for anyone. The last I heard, he refused to marry her and took off for good." She handed Irene back to Roma and picked up the papers on her desk, aligning all the corners with unnecessary care. "I doubt we'll see him here. Saquatucket caters more to the yacht crowd than we do."

"He might look you up."

Celia forced herself to laugh. "Roma, he probably doesn't even remember me. We were kids."

"Kids? I think not." Roma cocked her head and studied Celia until she blushed.

"Okay, we weren't kids. But we were really young. My life has changed completely since those days and I'm sure his has, too."

"Maybe." Roma didn't sound as if she believed it. But then she shrugged. "I'm off to the grocery store. I just have time for a quick run before I pick Blaine up from kindergarten."

Celia nodded, although another arrow of pain shot into her to nestle beside the first. Leo had been seven months younger than Blaine, but because of his October birthday he would have been a year behind in school. This would have been his last year at home with her. *Don't go there, Celia. You're not an at-*

home mom anymore. You're not a mom, period. Or a wife. You're just the harbormaster now.

''See you.'' Roma corralled her younger son and blew a kiss at Celia before she swept out the door.

Celia could only be grateful that her friend hadn't perceived her pain. Leaning both elbows on her desk as she sank into her chair again, she pressed the palms of her hands hard against her eyes, refusing to shed the tears that wanted to spring free.

After two and a half years she didn't think of them as much now, Milo and Leo. Only a few times a day as opposed to a few times a minute. The agony had faded to a dull ache—except for momentary flare-ups like this one. Often, they were triggered by Roma's three children. She suspected her friend knew it, because Roma didn't bring them around as much as she once had.

But Celia refused to crawl into a hole and hide for the rest of her life, which was what she'd have to do to avoid seeing children. She loved Roma's kids and her husband, Greg. She'd lost her own family but that was no reason to cut Roma's out of her life. Still, sometimes it was hard. Just…so *hard.*

She turned her mind away from the thoughts because she couldn't stand them anymore. Lord, she couldn't believe Roma's news.

Reese. On the same small piece of land with her. She'd given up all hope of ever seeing him again years ago. But before that…before that, there had been a time when Reese Barone had been so much a part of her that she'd never even imagined she could have a life that didn't include him.

Reese. Her first love, the boy with whom she'd spent a carefree long-ago summer making love and sailing every moment she wasn't working. Looking back, it was easy to see that she would never have fit into Reese Barone's world on a permanent basis. She had been a fisherman's daughter, a motherless girl who knew more about where the best stripers were than she did about fashion or feminine pursuits. She'd been seventeen to his twenty-one, a local Cape girl who'd only ever been to Boston on a high school field trip, inexperienced and easily won.

They couldn't have been more different. He was the grandson of a Sicilian immigrant whose ambition and drive had brought the Barone name both fortune and fame. Second of eight children in a large and loving family, Reese was born knowing how to make money. Well-traveled, confident, he'd had no lack of females vying for his attention. Why he'd been interested in her would always remain a mystery.

Reese. She'd heard rumors that he'd been disowned by his family years ago. He'd gotten a girl pregnant then refused to marry her. Had it been a girl like Celia, she had little doubt his prominent, wealthy family would have reacted with such ire. But the girl supposedly was a debutante whose family was close to the Barones, and his refusal to marry her had set off a Barone family explosion the reverberations of which had been heard clear up to the mid-Cape village of Harwichport where they made their summer home.

Reese. Ridiculously, it still hurt to think of him. Were his eyes still that beautiful shade of gray that could turn as silver as a dime or as stormy as a rough sea? Was his hair still long enough to blow in the ocean breezes that filled the sails?

Don't be silly, Celia. You remember a fantasy.

Maybe her memory had embellished on eyes that were really quite ordinary. Maybe the hair had silver in it now. Maybe that lean, whipcord body had softened and filled out a little too much. Maybe—

It didn't matter. He'd sailed away without a word to her after the news of his impending fatherhood had trickled out to the Cape from Boston. She'd been left with the realization that she'd meant nothing more to him than a little convenient summer sex. The only good thing she'd had to cling to was that he hadn't gotten her pregnant.

Although...

There was a tiny, traitorous part of her that had regretted, for a very long time, that he hadn't. He wouldn't have stayed, but she'd have had a little piece of him to hold on to.

That part of her had softened when she'd married Milo and had melted completely away after she'd finally gotten pregnant and had Leo. She couldn't honestly say she'd forgotten Reese, but she hadn't entertained any more thoughts of ever seeing him again.

Well, it was probably a moot point. She briskly straightened her papers again, then reached for the phone. She had work to do.

Thirty minutes later, one of the young men who worked for her at the marina skidded to a halt just inside her office door. "Hey, Mrs. P.! You gotta check this out! There's an eighty-footer coming in. I swear it looks brand new!"

Celia rose from her desk, quickly pasting a semblance of a smile on her face as the kid babbled on about the incoming yacht. Most of the staff had worked for Milo before she'd taken over, and she hated for them to see her blue. Their spirits rose and fell right along with hers.

She went to the door eagerly, glad for the distraction. The kid was easily impressed, but if he was right, she wanted to see the yacht. The young worker said it was one of the newest models available—and one of the costliest. Extraordinary wealth was common in the area around the Cape but a brand-new yacht built to spec from any of the top makers was worth a close look. If only to drool over.

Walking to the door of the shack, she stepped out onto the pier, shading her eyes from the morning sun as she squinted southeast toward the opening of the small harbor. The sleek silhouette of a cruiser glided in and she watched as one of her staff directed its captain to a slip then waited until the boat was tied up. A man leaped from the deck of the yacht to the pier and conferred with the dock worker for a moment, and she saw the boy pointing her way.

The man came striding up the pier toward her. He was tall and rangy, with wide shoulders and a lean, easy movement to him that would make a woman look twice. His dark hair gleamed in the sunlight—

And her heart dropped into her stomach where it promptly began doing backflips. The man coming up the pier was Reese Barone.

She barely had time to recover, to gather her stunned sensibilities into some semblance of a professional attitude. Thank God Roma had warned her that he was in the area.

"Hello," she called as he drew near. "You need a temp mooring?"

"I do. I'd really like to get a slip at the dock if you have one available for short term." The voice was very deep and very masculine, shivering along her hypersensitive nerve endings like the whisper of a feather over flesh. He extended a hand. "Celia. Dare I hope that you remember me?"

"Reese." She cleared her throat as she took his hand, giving it one quick squeeze before sliding hers free and tucking it into the pocket of her windbreaker. Was it her imagination that made her feel as if her palm was tingling where their hands had met? "Welcome to South Harwich. It's been a long time." There. Nice and noncommittal.

"Thirteen years."

She couldn't look at him. "Something like that."

"Exactly like that." There was almost a thread of anger in his low tone, and it startled her into looking at him. Instantly, she was sorry. His eyes weren't nearly as ordinary as she'd hoped, but as extraordinary as she'd remembered. Thick, dark lashes framed irises of gray. At the moment they looked as dark and stormy as his voice sounded. Crackling energy seemed to radiate from him. What could *he* have to be mad about? He was the one who'd taken off without a word.

"Mrs. Papaleo?" Angie, her office assistant, stuck her head out the door. "Maintenance is on the phone."

Maintenance. She needed to take the call. She had to get the fourth piling replaced; it hadn't been the same since that boat crashed into it on the Fourth. Angie could help Reese. Twenty-two and supremely capable, Angie Dunstan had worked for the marina since before Milo had died. Angie could charm a bird from its tree—and she'd be delighted to entertain Reese. Let her deal with him.

"I have to go," she said to Reese. "Come on in the office and Angie can show you what's available."

"You're the harbormaster?" There was a definite note of skepticism in his voice.

"Yes." A small thrill of pride lifted her chin as she turned and headed back up the pier. But she couldn't ignore the sensations that tingled through her as she walked. She could almost *feel* him behind her.

Well, it didn't matter. He'd asked for temp space, which meant he'd be gone again in a few days.

"How long have you had the job?" he asked from behind her.

She didn't turn around or slow down. "Over two years."

"Somebody retire? I can't even remember who worked this marina."

She was at the door of the office by now, and she took a deep breath, turning to meet his eyes squarely. And just as it had in the old days, her stomach fluttered when those gray eyes gazed into hers. "My father-in-law was the harbormaster for years," she said quietly. "When he died, my husband got the job. Then the selectmen offered it to me after Milo passed away."

"I heard you were widowed."

She nodded. God, how she hated that word.

"I'm sorry."

She saw something move in his eyes and she looked away quickly. Compassion from Reese, of all people, would do her in. "Angie, how about putting Mr. Barone in the Margolies' slip along pier four. They won't be back until May and they gave us permission to rent it out on a temp basis.'' She gave a perfunctory nod of her head without meeting his eyes again. ''Enjoy your stay.''

Enjoy your stay.

That night, lying in the stateroom of his boat, Reese's teeth ground together at the memory of Celia's glib words. She'd blown him off as easily as she had thirteen years ago. No, he corrected himself, even more easily. Last time, she'd had her father do it.

Father. That led to thoughts of other things she'd said. Father-*in-law*. He knew, on an intellectual level, that time had passed. But he didn't feel any older. And Celia still looked much the same. It was hard to believe she'd married and buried a husband since he'd seen her last.

Had she had something going with the Papaleo guy that summer while she'd been with him? His memory of this marina was vague, since his family had always kept their crafts at Saquatucket, but he could dimly recall the wiry Greek fellow who'd kept things in order years ago. He had an even less reliable memory of the man's son, no more than another wiry figure, possibly taller than the older man.

No. If she'd cheated on him, he'd have known it. He'd been sure of Celia back in those days. She'd been his. All his.

He swore, gritting his teeth for an entirely different reason as his body reacted to the memories, and flipped onto his back.

Celia. God, she'd been so beautiful she'd taken his breath away. Today had been no different. How could that be? After thirteen years she shouldn't look so damned good. She was thirty—he knew she'd just had a birthday at the end of September.

The thought pulled him up short. Why did he still remember the birthdate of a woman he'd slept with years ago for one brief summer?

She was your fantasy.

Yes, indeed. She had been his fantasy. At an age when a young man was particularly impressionable, Celia had been lithe, warm, adoring and pliable. If he'd suggested it, she'd rarely opposed him. She truly had been every man's dream. But that was all she'd been, he assured himself. A dream.

A dream that had evaporated like the morning mist over the harbor once she'd heard the false rumor about him and that girl from Boston.

An old wave of bitterness welled up. He didn't often allow himself to think about the last words he and his father had exchanged all those years ago. To people who asked, he merely said he had no family.

And he didn't. He'd never opened nor answered the letters from his mother or his brothers and sisters, mostly because there was nothing to say. He hadn't done a damn thing wrong, and he had nothing to apologize for. Nick had been the most persistent. Reese bet he'd gotten fifteen letters from his big brother in those first five years or so. There were probably more out there floating around. He'd sailed from place to place so much there would have been no way to predict his movements or the places he might have chosen to dock.

On the other hand, he'd never received so much as a single line from his father. That was all it would have taken, too. One line. *I'm sorry.*

He exhaled heavily. Why in the hell was he thinking about that tonight? It was ancient history. He had a family of his own now, was a very different person than he'd been more than a decade ago.

The thought brought Amalie to mind and he smiled to himself. He'd never pictured himself as a father, and he certainly wouldn't recommend acquiring a child the way she'd come into his life, but he loved her dearly. If he could love a child who wasn't even biologically his so much, what would it be like to have a child of his own?

As if she'd been waiting for the chance, Celia sprang into his head again. He was more than mildly shocked when he realized that, subconsciously, he'd always pictured her in the role of his imaginary child's mother. Dammit! He was *not* going to waste any more time thinking about that faithless woman.

Throwing his legs over the side of his bunk, he yanked on a pair of ragged jeans and a sweatshirt and stomped through the rest of his living space to the stairs. On deck, he idly picked up a pair of binoculars and scanned the horizon. Nothing interesting, only one small fishing boat. A careless captain, too, he observed, running without lights.

Casually he swung the binoculars around to the shoreline. The area had been developed considerably since he'd been gone, as had the whole Cape and the rest of the Eastern seaboard. A lot of new houses, some right on the water. The only place that would still be undisturbed completely would be the Cape Cod National Seashore on the Outer Cape, but here along the Lower Cape he couldn't see that.

The quiet sound of a small, well-tuned motor reached his ears and he glanced back toward the south. The little boat he'd seen was coming in, still without lights. Then the motor cut out and he saw the flash of oars. Why would the guy kill his power before he reached the dock?

The quiet *plish* of the oars came nearer. The boat was close enough that he could now see it easily without the binoculars, then closer still, and he realized the guy intended to put in right here at the marina.

There appeared to be only one sailor aboard, and a small one at that. Probably a teenager flouting the rules, which would explain his cutting the motor early and trying to sneak in. The boy tied up his boat and caught a ladder one-handed, nimbly climbing to the dock while carrying a fishing cooler in his other hand.

Reese grasped the smooth mahogany rail of his boat and vaulted over the edge onto the dock. He walked toward the boy, intending to give him a rough education in proper night lighting, but just then the boy walked beneath one of the floodlights that illuminated the marina.

The "boy" was Celia daSilva. No, not daSilva. Papaleo.

"Celia!" He didn't even stop to think. "What the hell do you think you're doing? Of all the irresponsible, un—"

"Shh!" He'd clearly startled her, but she recovered quickly. She ran toward him, making next to no noise in her practical dockside slip-ons. Before he could utter another syllable, she clapped one small hand over his mouth.

Reese wasn't a giant but he was a lot bigger than Celia, and the action brought her body perilously close to his. He could feel the heat of her, was enveloped in a smell so familiar it catapulted him instantly back in time to a day when he'd had the right to pull that small, lithe figure against him. His palms itched with the urge to do exactly that and he rubbed them against the sides of his jeans, trying to master the images that flooded his mind.

Her eyes were wide and dark, bled of any color in the deep shadow thrown by the angle at which she was standing. But he could see that she recognized the familiarity of their proximity almost as fast as he did.

"I can explain," she whispered, her voice a breath of sound. "Just don't make any more noise."

The words had barely left her mouth when a light snapped on aboard a nearby yacht. "Mrs. Papaleo? Is that you?"

It was a deep, slightly accented male voice. Reese felt the vibration as the man leaped onto the dock, much as he had a moment before, and walked toward them.

"Don't say *anything,*" Celia warned. To his astonishment, her hand cupped his jaw, sliding along it so that her thumb almost grazed the corner of his lips. At the same time he felt her bump his hip with the cooler she still carried. He lifted his own hands automatically, curling his fingers around the handle, over hers and putting his other hand at her waist. A part of him registered the fact that the cooler felt a lot lighter than it should if it was full of fish. But a larger part of him was much more attentive to Celia's proximity, the way her soft hand felt curled under his and the way her palm cupped his jaw. Her hands were warm and he knew the slender body concealed beneath the wind shirt and jeans would be even warmer. Even softer.

She waited the barest instant until the man walking toward them couldn't help but see the intimate pose, then she slowly stepped away a pace, letting her hands slide off him as if reluctant to let him go despite the interruption.

"Hello, Mr. Tiello," she said. "It's me. This is, uh, an old friend. Reese Barone. Reese, Ernesto Tiello."

Reese stepped forward and extended his hand automatically, trying to ignore his racing pulse. What was she up to? She'd deliberately made it sound as if he were a very *good* old friend. "Nice to meet you."

"And you, sir." Tiello was a bulky fellow, probably ten years older than Reese himself, with a heavy accent that might indicate nonnative roots. The man looked from one to the other of them. "Were you out on the water?"

"Yes." Celia turned to face Tiello. Her free hand reached for and found Reese's and she intertwined their fingers. "A little night fishing. We used to do it all the time when we were young."

A gleam of amusement lit the dark eyes and Tiello smiled. "I see."

Reese felt his own lips twitch as he fought not to chuckle. Celia was going to be sorry she started this.

Another boat light along the dock snapped on. "I thought I heard your voice, Ernesto." The voice was feminine, smoky and suggestive. It instantly made a man wonder if the woman attached to it lived up to its promise.

Tiello's tanned features creased into what Reese assumed was a seductive smile. "It is, indeed, and I'm flattered that you thought of me, Claudette."

A form leaped from the deck of the yacht from which the light shone. Backlit by the brightness, the woman appeared tall and slender. Then she drew closer. She had blond hair caught in a thick braid that trailed over one shoulder so far that Reese knew if it was unbound her hair would reach her hips. Big blue eyes, a heart-shaped face and a slight cleft in her chin added even more interest to her pretty face, but the mouth changed it all. "Pretty" became "sexy as hell" at the first glimpse of those lips.

"Hello," she purred, extending her hand and favoring him with a brilliant smile that revealed small, perfect white teeth. "I'm Claudette Mason."

"Reese Barone." He repeated the ritual he'd just completed with Tiello, who was wearing a distinctly sulky look on his face.

"Did you just arrive?" Her gaze drifted over him. "I'm sure I would have noticed if you'd been here earlier."

"I docked a few hours ago." Celia's fingers had gone stiff and uncooperative in his; he glanced down at her but she was wearing an absolutely expressionless mask that would have served her well in a poker game.

"I hope you'll be here for a while. We could get to know each other." Claudette had yet to acknowledge Celia's presence, let alone the fact that he was holding her hand.

"Er, thanks," he said, "but I'll be occupied while I'm here." He dragged Celia's hand up with his to display their entwined fingers. "Celia and I haven't seen each other in a while and we have a lot to catch up on."

"Ah. I see." Claudette Mason made a moue of regret. Without even a pause, she turned back to

Tiello. "Could I interest you in a drink, Ernesto? Mr. Brevery has gone to Boston for the night."

The man's face brightened as if she'd brought him a gift. "I would be delighted," he said. He turned to Celia and Reese. "Very nice to meet you, Mr. Barone. Have a lovely evening, Mrs. Papaleo."

"Thank you. You do the same." Celia tugged discreetly at the hand he'd lowered, but he kept her fingers imprisoned in his. "Are you ready to go, Reese?"

As the other pair walked back down the dock toward the woman's yacht—the *Golden Glow,* he noted—he lifted a brow and looked down at Celia. "Sure." In a lower voice, he added, "But it might be nice if I knew where I was supposed to be going."

"You'll have to walk home with me." Celia sounded grumpy and grudging as they moved out of range of the other couple, and he felt his own surly mood creeping back over him. "I guess I owe you an explanation."

Reese nodded. "I guess." Sarcasm colored his tone as he allowed her to tow him along the dock toward the street.

"Thank you," she said curtly. "I appreciate you going along with my...my..."

"Deception?" he offered pleasantly. "Fabrication? How about lie?"

They were walking along the edge of the harbor now and as she turned onto a street away from the marina, Celia yanked her hand free. "There's a good reason." Her voice sounded defensive.

"I imagine so," he said, allowing the cutting edge in his voice to slice, "since I can't think of any reason you'd want to hold my hand after dumping me thirteen years ago.''

"*I* dumped *you?*" Celia stopped in her tracks. "Excuse me, but I seem to recall you being the one who dropped off the face of the earth." Then she started walking again, fast, and despite his superior size, he had to take large strides to catch up with her. "Why are we arguing? As you pointed out, it's ancient history. It doesn't matter anymore."

He could feel the anger slipping free of his control and he clamped down on it, gritting his teeth to prevent another retort. It made him remember gritting his teeth in a very similar manner—but for a very different reason—just a short while ago, and he pulled up a vivid mental image of himself smacking the heel of his hand against his forehead. *How stupid would I have to be,* he lectured himself, *to care about what happened when we were still practically kids?* He wasn't any more interested than she was in resurrecting their old relationship.

"No," he said softly, definitely. "It doesn't matter anymore."

They walked in awkward silence for a few hundred yards.

"Who's Mr. Brevery?" It was an abrupt change of topic but he wanted to show her how little he cared about the past.

Celia cleared her throat. "Claudette's employer. He's put up here every October for at least a half dozen years."

"And Tiello?"

Her mouth twisted. "Playboy. Too much money and too much time to waste. This is the third year he's visited us in the fall."

The same probably applied to him in her estima-
tion. So what? He'd stopped caring what Celia
thought of him long ago. "So why were you out on
the water with no lights?"

She looked around and he realized she was checking to be sure no one was near. "I'd rather tell you
when we're inside."

Inside. She was going to invite him into her house.
Although he knew she was only doing it because
she'd entangled him in whatever little scheme she was
up to, he still felt a quickening interest, as if he were
still a teenage boy who saw a chance to score.

*She broke your heart, remember? You're not inter-
ested.*

*Right. That's why you came back after you stopped
by Saquatucket in late August and found out she was
still around.*

"Here," she said. She pushed open a gate in a low
picket fence and led the way up a crushed-shell path
to the door of a boxy Cape Cod farmhouse-style
home. The place clearly was an old Cape treasure.
She paused on the stoop to unlock the door, then
pushed it open and beckoned to him without meeting
his eyes. "Please come in."

Formal. She was nervous. About having him
around? About what he'd interrupted? He told himself
it didn't matter. "Nice place," he said. When she was
young, she'd lived in one of the most modest cottages
on the Cape. This house probably was on the historic
register.

The living room was furnished with heavy pieces
in shades of creams and browns, with an irregularly
shaped glass coffee table mounted atop a large piece
of driftwood. Over the mantel hung a painting of the

harbor as it must have looked a hundred years ago, with small fishing boats moored along the water's edge, stacks of lobster pots and nets piled haphazardly and a shell path leading to small, boxy cottages similar to the one in which he stood. There was a bowl filled with dried cranberries on the coffee table, and as he watched, she switched on additional lights.

"Thank you." She hesitated. "It was my husband's family home for four generations."

"Your husband the harbormaster."

"Yes." She sounded faintly defensive. "Would you like something to drink?"

"No." He flopped down into a comfortably overstuffed chair without invitation. "I'd like an explanation."

Two

Celia took a deep, nervous breath, trying to calm the fluttering muscles of her stomach. What on earth had possessed her to involve Reese in this mess? She'd reacted instinctively, knowing she'd had no time to waste. And knowing Reese was safe. The one thing she did know was that he couldn't possibly be involved. That would have required him to be in the area in the last few years.

"I was looking for drug smuggling activity."

"Drug smugglers?" He sounded incredulous. The faint air of hostility she'd sensed from him disappeared as he sat up straight and stared at her.

She perched on the edge of the couch and clasped her hands together. "It's imperative that none of the clients along the dock learn about it."

"Why?"

"It's possible that someone moored here could be a part of a drug operation."

"So when I came along and blew the whistle, you decided to use me as a cover?" Reese's eyes were intent, unsmiling.

She shrugged. "I didn't know what else to do. You were shouting loud enough to wake folks on the other side of town."

The side of his mouth twitched, as if he were struggling not to smile. "Sorry." He leaned back against the rough fabric of the chair, stretched out his long legs, then looked at her skeptically. "Drug smuggling?"

She popped up off the couch, uncomfortable with his questions and annoyed at the derisive tone. "I'm not crazy," she said defensively. "You'd be amazed at the amount of illegal stuff that goes on around here."

He laughed aloud, but she had the sense that he was laughing at her rather than with her. "I've been in dozens of harbors along dozens of shorelines and, believe me, I've seen more kinds of 'illegal stuff' than you could imagine. I'm just wondering what you think you can do about it."

"Maybe nothing." She carefully looked past him, hoping her face wasn't too transparent.

"Celia." He waited until she reluctantly dragged her gaze back to mesh with his. "You could be putting yourself in serious danger. Drug runners are criminals. They wouldn't think twice about hurting you if they caught you spying on them. Leave the investigation to the law enforcement guys who get paid to do it."

She wanted to laugh, an entirely inappropriate reaction, and she bit the inside of her lip hard. If he only knew! "I'll be careful," she said.

"Careful isn't good enough." His tone was harsh. "Do you think I'm kidding about getting hurt? This isn't a game—"

"I know it's not!" Her voice overrode his. "They killed my husband and my son." *Dear God, help me.* She couldn't believe she'd blurted that out.

The words hung in the air, still stunning her after two years. She collapsed again on the couch like a balloon that had lost its helium, putting her face in her hands. An instant later she realized that Reese's weight was settling onto the cushions beside her.

"I'm sorry," he said. A large, warm hand settled on her back and rubbed gentle circles as if she were a baby in need of soothing. "I am so sorry, Celia. I didn't know."

"I didn't expect you would." She pressed the heels of her palms hard against her eyes, pushing back the tears. She wasn't a crier; tears accomplished nothing but making you feel like you needed a nap to recharge the batteries you drained bawling. "It was just local news." *Except to me.*

There was a small silence. "Tell me what happened."

She hadn't spoken of it in a long time. Not even to Roma, who she knew worried over her silence. But for some reason, she felt compelled to talk tonight. Maybe it was because she had a certain degree of familiarity with Reese due to their shared past. Maybe it was because he hadn't known her family and therefore could be less emotionally involved. Most likely it was because she knew he wouldn't be around long and it wouldn't matter.

Drawing in a deep breath, she sighed heavily and shifted back against the couch, her hands falling limp in her lap. Reese sat close, his arm now draped along the back of the couch behind her shoulders. It should have bothered her, but the numbness that had been so familiar in that first horrible year of her bereavement was with her again, and she couldn't work up the energy to mind.

"We only had been married for two years when Milo's dad passed away and Milo was asked to take over as harbormaster. He'd been raised on the pier and he knew the work already." She smiled briefly, looking into the past. "He was good at it. Everybody liked Milo."

Reese didn't speak, although she saw him nod encouragingly in her peripheral vision.

"Our son was born three years later. We named him Emilios, like his father and grandfather. Leo was his nickname. I had worked at the marina but I stayed home with him after he was born." The numbness was fading and she concentrated on breathing deeply and evenly, forming the words with care. Anything to keep from letting the words shred her heart again.

"When Leo was two, Milo mentioned to me that he thought there was something funny going on down toward Monomoy Island. One night in September he came home and told me he'd called the FBI, that he was pretty certain some kind of illegal contraband was being brought ashore."

"That was smart." Reese's voice was quiet.

"He didn't know what else to do," she said. "After he showed them where he thought the action was happening, he stayed away. The federal agents got a lot of information from him and that was it. Almost a year passed and nothing happened that we knew of. We figured they probably were proceeding cautiously, starting some kind of undercover operation. And then one day Milo took Leo with him on an errand over to Nantucket. Halfway across the sound, their boat exploded.''

Reese swore vividly. "What happened?"

She took another deep, careful breath. "At first I assumed it was an accident. Just a horrible, awful accident. And then federal agents came around one day and told me there had been an explosive device attached to the bottom of the boat. It had been detonated by someone close enough to see them go out on the water.''

She stopped speaking and there was silence in the room, broken only by the steady tick-tock of the old captain's clock Milo's father had restored. She wound it every morning when she came downstairs.

"How old was your—Leo?"

Her heart shrank from the question. She could deal with this if she just didn't think too much about it. But she couldn't talk about Leo. She just couldn't. "Two and a half. He would have started kindergarten next year." Her voice quavered. *Shut up, shut up. Stop talking.* "He was very blond, like I was as a child, and he had big velvety-brown eyes. He adored his daddy and there was nothing he loved better than going out on the…the boat w-with Milo." Her voice was beginning to hitch as sobs forced their way out.

She felt Reese's arms come hard around her, pulling her to his chest as the floodgates of long-suppressed grief opened. "Shh." His voice came dimly through the storm of agony that swept over her.

"I wish—I w-wish I'd died, too." She stuffed a

fist in her mouth, appalled at voicing the thought that had lived in her head since the terrible day she'd buried her husband and her baby boy.

"Shh," he said again. "I know." She felt a big hand thread through her hair, cupping her scalp and gently massaging. He'd done that years ago, she remembered, when she'd been upset with her father's reaction to him the day she'd introduced them.

Abruptly, it was all too much. Her father, her family, Reese…

She cried for a long, long time. Reese did nothing, simply held her while she soaked the front of his sweatshirt with tears. At one point he reached over to the end table and snagged a box of tissues—probably afraid she'd use his shirt to blow her nose—but he didn't let go of her and as soon as he handed her a tissue he put his arm around her again.

His hands were big and warm and comforting. His arms made her feel ridiculously secure. She hadn't allowed herself to lean on anyone in so long….

Reese tilted his head and glanced down at the sleeping woman in his arms. He'd been shaken to the core by her flat recital earlier. His problems, his *issues* with his family, seemed petty in comparison.

Not for the first time, he wondered if his parents were still living, if his siblings were all right. Some of them might be married now. For all he knew, he could be an uncle. He'd frozen them forever in his mind, but they'd moved on with their lives just as he had.

Although he really hadn't. In more than a dozen years he'd done nothing of note besides win a few silly boat races here and there. He'd made plenty of money and given a lot of it away, but he couldn't think of one single lasting thing of importance that he'd leave behind if he died tomorrow. Except Amalie, and he couldn't take credit for her.

Celia must feel like that, too. Only it must be worse knowing that she *had* had something lasting and it was gone. A steady relationship and a child to carry on her genes—yes, it was much worse for her. He was sure her marriage had been good, just from the way she uttered her husband's name, as if the mere speaking of it could evoke warm, fond feelings of affection. A ridiculous feeling of jealousy swept through him. She wasn't his, hadn't been his for years. She'd chosen another man. And yes, she'd definitely had something lasting…until it had been ripped away from her in one brutal moment.

Jealousy faded beneath compassion and pity. *I wish I'd died, too.* What would it be like to lose the people you loved most in the world? Particularly the child. God, losing someone close to you, a friend, was bad enough, as he well knew. And he had firsthand experience with a child who'd lost her parents. But to have your child go before you— He shivered, thinking of his adopted six-year-old daughter, Amalie, a bright butterfly flitting through his life, bringing radiant colors to his days. It wasn't natural for any child to die and there was no way to accept it. He couldn't even imagine what he would do if he ever lost Ammie.

And she wasn't even his. Well, she was now, thanks to the adoption laws of the State of Florida. But her parents had been his best racing buddy, Kent, and his wife, Julie. They'd died at sea before Amalie's second birthday and he'd been called on to honor his pledge to be Amalie's godfather in a far more intimate way than any of them ever had expected.

He lifted one hand and wearily rubbed his temples. He needed to call down to the Keys where he'd made his home, to check in with Velva, his housekeeper, nanny and surrogate mother all rolled into one, to talk to Amalie. This was the first time he'd left her in the four years since her parents had died and he hadn't been sure it was a good idea. But Velva and Amalie's teacher both had urged him to take a few weeks for himself. He hadn't sailed anywhere alone since Kent and Julie had died and he'd finally let himself be talked into this vacation. He'd decided to have one last carefree fling before selling the cruiser. He was a man who had responsibilities now. No more world-cruising for him.

One carefree fling? Ha. The minute you heard Celia was still around, you made plans to come back up here and see her for yourself.

He pulled his head back farther to look at Celia. Hard to believe she was lying here in his arms, even if it was only because she needed comfort. She'd wept silently, her slender body set in tense denial as huge tears rolled down her cheeks and soaked the fabric of both their shirts, until he'd told her to stop holding it in. And then she'd finally broken. She'd let him draw her against his chest and she'd sobbed and sobbed. Awful, desolate sounds that had made his own throat ache. How the hell long had it been since she'd let herself cry? Surely the woman had friends, if not family, around. She'd lived here all her life.

But there was something almost austere about Celia now that she hadn't had when she was young. The woman she was now didn't need people—or didn't *want* to need them, he'd bet. The woman she'd been when he'd known her, a flower just in the first fresh moments of full bloom, had had no such boundaries. She'd been free with her hugs and her bright silvery laughter; her face had been open and alive, always smiling. And when she'd seen him coming, that smile had lit up the world.

As he thought of the girl he'd known, another memory floated through his head. It wasn't of the first time they'd made love. Though he could remember that, too. She'd been a virgin and it hadn't been particularly fun for her, he suspected, although she'd never told him so, and she'd made him feel like the king of the world.

No, the memory that haunted him was of an entirely different time....

"Reese! It's the middle of summer a-and it's broad daylight. There are tourists everywhere!"

He laughed, enjoying the way her eyes widened when he took her hand and pulled her down onto the deck of the catamaran, his purpose clear. It was a small boat with no cabin, but it did have a low railing around the deck. If they were careful... He'd fantasized about making love to Celia under the bright summer sun since the first time they'd been together more than two months ago.

"This little bay is fairly private, though." He slid his hands over her bare, tanned torso, gently tugging at the strings that tied her bikini top into place until he could toss the scrap of cloth aside. "It's an unwritten law of the sea. You never approach a moored boat if you've hailed them and nobody answers."

Her finely arched eyebrows rose. "I can think of a dozen times I've broken that rule myself."

But she wasn't really arguing with him. Her small hands ran lightly up his arms, over the swell of his biceps and onto his shoulders, and she shivered, falling silent as he flicked his thumbs over her nipples, bringing them to beautiful taut points. He'd never seen her before in bright light and her skin was so satiny, her peaks and valleys so smoothly curved, that she literally stopped his breath.

"Celia." He breathed her name as if it were a prayer, finding her mouth with easy familiarity, feeling the thrill that always shot through him at her instant response.

"I love you." Her words were a whisper of sound, barely audible as he nibbled his way along her jaw, then slid his mouth down the tender column of her neck, pressing kisses to the delicate arch of her collarbone. He trailed his tongue along her skin, catching the faint scent that wasn't perfume but merely the essence of her.

"You're so beautiful." His palms cupped the sweet weight of her breasts and he drew back just far enough to feast his eyes on the soft, feminine flesh he'd uncovered. Her nipples were a glowing coppery color, begging him to taste them, and he leaned down again, touching her with his tongue, lightly at first, then tugging her fully into his mouth to suckle one tender tip until she arched against him, twisting and crying out.

Smiling against her skin, he released one tight nubbin and blew on it. Celia's eyes flew open. "Reese…" Her hands had been clutching his shoulders. Dragging them down over his chest, she in-

dulged in a little teasing of her own, running her fin-
gers through the dark mat of hair that spread across
his breastbone and arrowed downward. She touched
his flat nipples, rubbing small circles, making his
breath come faster as the sensation triggered an even
more intense need within him.

As she trailed one finger down along the ribbon of
hair to his navel and beyond, he stripped out of his
bathing suit one-handed and kicked it away without
leaving her. The mere act of freeing himself from the
restrictions of clothing turned him on even more as
he felt the warm air move over him, the sun hot on
his back. All that lay between them now was one tiny
piece of fabric. He stroked her ribs, her hips, her
belly, moving slowly down her body, savoring her. He
loved the feel of every smooth inch. His finger
skimmed the delicate dip of her navel and farther,
over her hipbone and down to where the elastic of
her bathing suit bottom impeded his exploration.

With slow, deliberate motions, he slipped a finger
beneath the elastic and ran it back and forth, then
delved a bit deeper until his long fingers combed
through the dense mat of curls between her legs. She
was dewed and slippery, and she arched beneath him,
one long silken leg curving up over his hip and pull-
ing him hard against her. They both made small
sounds of delight as their bodies reacted to the sweet
pressure.

Gently, reluctantly, he slid away from her long
enough to hook his fingers in the fabric and pull it
down and off. Celia watched him, her breath rushing
in and out, but as the sun poured over her gloriously
naked body, she made a motion to cover herself with
her hands. "This makes me feel…exposed."

He chuckled, lowering himself to her, taking her wrists and pulling them up beside her shoulders as he covered her. He shifted, snuggling himself firmly into the cleft of her thighs, groaning a little at the exquisite pressure that resulted from sandwiching himself between them. "Is this better?"

She smiled up at him, her lips quivering slightly. "Yes. But what if someone—"

He covered her mouth with his own again, using his tongue to draw a response from her until she was fully engaged in the kiss. When he released her wrists she clasped his shoulders, clinging to him, pressing her bare flesh against his chest and making him growl with approval. He worked one hand between their bodies, bypassing his straining flesh in favor of the soft fleece that hid her feminine secrets. Slowly, slowly, he inched one finger down, until he felt the pouting bump beneath his finger. Equally slowly, he pressed and circled gently, ignoring his body's urgent demands until she was writhing and frantic beneath him.

"Reese," she begged him, tearing her mouth from his. "Reese…"

"What, baby?" He used the moment to push his hand farther between her thighs, loving the slick, moist heat and the fact that he'd been the one to make her respond that way. "Do you want me?"

She nodded, reaching one small hand down to encircle him. He groaned as an involuntary surge of excitement threatened his self-control. She'd only recently gotten brave enough to touch him but she was a fast learner and the mere thought of what she could do to him— Under the circumstances, he thought, it might not be such a good idea. As she traced one finger across the sensitive tip, he reared back, removing himself from her grasp. He set his hands on her inner thighs, pressing them apart and looking at the secret treasure they yielded.

Celia reached for him, her modesty all but forgotten. "Hurry…"

He was dragged from his reverie by Celia's hand, which he held loosely in his, slowly rising to tuck her hair away from her face. It was only quick thinking that kept him from pulling her hand down to palm the hard ridge pushing at the front of his pants. Her eyelids fluttered as she stretched and he caught his breath, further aroused by both the memory and the soft slide of her body against his. Then her eyes opened and she blinked at him. "Reese." She didn't sound surprised, only cordial and a bit wary. "What time is it?"

He glanced at the old clock that had faithfully announced the hour as well as the half all night long. "Nearly six. Sleep well?"

"Nearly six?" She tried to shove herself upright. "Oh, no! You were here all night."

"Yeah." He held her easily in place though he was careful not to settle her too snugly into his lap. There was no way she could miss the evidence that would betray his thoughts if she lay against him any more closely. "Relax," he said, stroking her back. "All we did was sleep. Literally."

"Yes, but—"

"And you *did* make sure those folks down on the pier knew that I was coming home with you, remember? This will just make your story more convincing."

She stopped pushing against him, but her body felt stiff. It made him realize just how much he'd liked having her draped bonelessly over him in slumber. They'd never slept together all night way back when...and he was reminded of his daydream before she woke.

Without giving himself time to think, he asked, "Do you remember the first time we did it on the boat? We fell asleep afterward and my butt got sunburned."

"Reese!" A startled half laugh burst out of her and she sat up again, pushing herself away from him as he reluctantly let her go. "What brought that on?"

He shrugged, wishing he'd kept his mouth shut. "I was thinking about that summer." He didn't need to clarify. "So do you?"

"Do I what?"

"Remember."

She was avoiding his eyes. "Yes," she said quietly. "I remember."

"That was the first time we ever made love on a boat." He was gratified to see that she was breathing fast, her breasts rising and falling rapidly beneath her soft T-shirt. Oh, yeah. She remembered.

"I don't want to talk about this." She shot off the couch and stood over him, rubbing her arms briskly as if she were cold and her velvety-brown eyes held a determined look. "Are you leaving?"

She wanted to get rid of him. His pleasure in teasing her died instantly and he narrowed his eyes. "Aren't you going to offer me breakfast?"

"I have to grab a shower and get down to the pier. We have a couple of charters going out early this morning."

He decided he should get a gold star for not suggesting that they shower together. "All right," he said. "You go shower and I'll make breakfast. You have to eat or you'll feel bad."

Celia stood for a moment and he could almost see the argument going on in her head. If she let him in her kitchen while she showered, that would be a little more intimacy than she wanted. No, a lot more. But she'd been raised to be polite, and tossing him out without breakfast after he'd gone along with her story last night wouldn't set well with her conscience.

Finally she said, "All right. Thank you," in a tone so grudging that he nearly laughed aloud before she turned and walked out of the room without another word.

Reese got up and walked toward her kitchen, stopping at a little bathroom he found beneath the stairs on the way. The kitchen was shadowed in the first rays of dawn coming from a skylight that added a contemporary cachet to the old house. It was a charming combination of modern practicality and Cape Cod history, with Nantucket baskets and copper pots, a bowl of polished sea glass and shells. Two elegant seascapes graced the walls, and she'd laid hand-woven rugs and placemats, while a stunning wreath of cranberry and local greens hung above the old fireplace that now boasted a gas inset. His little village girl had done well for herself with her marriage.

Another image of Celia from all those years ago, standing on the dock waiting for him, flashed through his head as he started her coffeepot. God, how he'd loved her. Only a very young man could be that deeply, head-over-heels infatuated with a woman.

He'd never felt anything remotely like it since, never expected to again. That kind of feeling couldn't last.

Could it?

Of course not. He didn't harbor any feelings for Celia anymore, and surely he would if that wild, exuberant, bone-deep infatuation had really been love.

Sure. That's why you came flying over to this marina when the guys at Saquatucket told you she was harbormaster here now.

Simple curiosity. He'd wanted to see how she'd aged. At first he'd almost been disappointed to find that she looked nearly as youthful as she had the last time he'd seen her. He would always carry that image in his mind, because at the time, he hadn't realized they'd never be together again. She'd been waving wildly from the dock as he'd taken the cat back to his family's summer house, her slender body still warm from his caresses, lips swollen and eyes languorous as her hair streamed back from her face.

She still looked youthful, and initially he'd thought how little she'd changed. But as he'd drawn closer, changes had indeed been evident. She was slightly fuller in the breast and hip than she'd once been, a becoming difference. But the once-mobile lips were compressed, reluctant to curve into a smile, and her beautiful, soft, doe eyes were shadowed with secrets he couldn't decipher. The girl had become a woman—an extraordinarily lovely woman—but her coming of age clearly hadn't been smooth.

Upon the heels of the mild disappointment had been relief…and, if he was brutally truthful, an unkind pleasure that life hadn't been all roses and moonlight for her.

And then she'd told him about her family and any

lingering self-righteousness had fled in the face of the horror and sympathy her story evoked. He'd reached for her without thinking and it had felt so right when she'd come into his arms. So right that he'd been sorely tempted to jump her bones the next morning, like a total cad. Which he wasn't.

Okay, you might have been noble this morning, but you wouldn't say no to another close encounter, pal.

No. No, he wouldn't. In fact, he could easily imagine staying the night with Celia—or having her snuggled in his queen berth aboard the yacht—every night while he was moored here in Harwichport.

He thought about her as he surveyed the contents of the refrigerator, withdrew two cinnamon buns and put them in the microwave. He should be grateful to her for showing him that what they'd shared hadn't been real, even though it had hurt like hell at the time. She'd been the one who had made him realize that there was no such thing as real love. But he still *liked* her, just as a friend. And there was still an undeniable attraction between them....

He had three weeks' vacation left, if he didn't give in to the ridiculous urge to rush back to his daughter. Who, he reminded himself wryly, hadn't seemed in the least perturbed at the idea of her adoptive father going on an extended trip. That was a good thing, he knew from talking with the counselor he'd consulted periodically since Kent and Julie had died. Ammie felt as secure and comfortable as any other well-adjusted kid with only one parent.

So that, at least, wasn't something he had to worry about. It felt good—no, great—not to be worrying about Amalie. That was probably why Velva had kicked him out. She'd known he was far more apprehensive about a separation than his child would be.

So the bottom line was, his daughter would do fine without him for a few more weeks. Which meant he had plenty of time. He'd originally intended to stop briefly on the Cape, just to see how it had changed in the years since he'd been gone.

At least, that was what he'd told himself. But now, standing in Celia's kitchen in the light of early morning, having held her in his arms throughout the night, he had to face the truth. He'd come back to find her.

He'd never imagined she might be single, or perhaps he hadn't allowed himself to hope so, anyway. But she was. And so was he, and perhaps it was inevitable that they'd be drawn together again. After all, they shared a past no one else could ever take from them. She still felt comfortable with him at some elemental level she had yet to acknowledge or she never would have fallen asleep in his arms last night.

As he searched for napkins, mugs and plates, he thought about how revealing her actions had been. And he thought about how he'd felt as he'd held her in his arms again. It was difficult to admit he'd never gotten her out of his system. And he suspected that he had never been completely out of hers.

The telephone rang, interrupting his mental speculation. His eyebrows rose as he glanced at the clock. Damn early for a casual caller. He hoped nothing was wrong. It rang a second time, then a third. He couldn't hear the shower running anymore but he didn't hear Celia running for the phone, either. Did she have an answering machine? After the fifth ring, he decided she might not. With a mental shrug, he reached for the phone. She wanted people to think they were having a fling anyway, didn't she?

"Hello?"

There was dead silence on the other end of the line. Then, "I beg your pardon. I believe I have a wrong number." It was a quavery yet regal female voice, definitely a bit long in the tooth.

"Are you trying to reach Celia Papaleo?" He'd had time to practice the sound of it on the short trip from one marina to the other yesterday after he'd learned she was still around, but married.

"Why, yes," the caller was saying. "I am looking for Mrs. Papaleo. Is this her residence?"

"Yes, ma'am, it is. May I take a message?"

"Yes, you may. Might I ask to whom I am speaking?" If this old dame wasn't an English teacher in her day, he'd eat his shorts.

"This is Reese Barone, ma'am." The courtesy came naturally; he'd been drilled in it as a child and even suffered through etiquette classes where he and his brothers had been forced to dance with obnoxious little girls and to practice manners.

"Well, Mr. Barone, my name is Hilda Manguard and I am the chairwoman of the Harwich Historical Society. I would like you to pass along the following message to Mrs. Papaleo. Ask her to return my call and confirm that she will bring over the wreaths that she's making for our annual Autumn House Tour. Please tell her that I apologize for calling so early but I've been trying to contact her without success all week." And the old lady rattled off her number while Reese scrambled to find a pencil.

Just as he set the telephone back in the cradle, he heard a sound. He turned to find Celia standing in the doorway glaring at him. She wore jeans and a T-shirt beneath a V-necked fleece sweater designed to ward off the early morning chill. Her hair was slicked back from her face and already appeared to be half dry—which might explain why she hadn't heard the phone ring.

"Hey," he said, as if she weren't looking like she'd enjoy skinning him. "You have a message."

"What are you doing answering my phone?" she demanded.

"You didn't," he said. "And your machine didn't kick on."

"I don't have one." She practically snarled the words as she stalked toward him and snatched up the piece of paper on which he'd written the message. "Great. Now everybody on the Cape will know you were at my house at six in the morning."

"Was she an English teacher?"

Celia looked at him blankly. "Who?"

"Mrs. Manguard. She sounded like an English teacher."

"Miss. And yes, she was a long time ago. Then she became the principal of one of the elementary schools until she retired about twenty years ago." She pointed to one of the two places he'd set at the table. "Sit. Eat. And then you're leaving."

He nodded, figuring he'd pressed his luck far enough. "All right."

As she slipped into the seat across from him, he said, "So where are these wreaths you're making for the historical society?"

"Oh, no!" She mimed smacking her palm against her forehead, then snatched up the note she'd laid on the table and hastily scanned it. "I forgot all about those wreaths. Why did I say I'd do that?'' she asked herself.

''I take it this project isn't quite finished?''

''It isn't even *started*. I agreed to donate ten wreaths. They hang them in the homes on their annual house tour and sell chances on some of them. At the conclusion of the tour, the winners are drawn.'' She wiped cinnamon glaze from her fingertips. ''And they want them on Saturday.''

''Today is Thursday.''

''I know that.'' From the tone of her voice, his helpfulness wasn't appreciated.

''Are they cranberry wreaths like the one in your living room?''

''Some are. Others are made of marsh grasses and decorated with shells. Ack! And I'm out of marsh grass. Sometime before this evening I've got to get my hands on more.'' She sighed. ''This is *not* going to be a good day.''

''And that includes the way it started?'' he asked wryly.

Her troubled gaze met his across the table. ''Reese, I do appreciate you letting me cry all over you last night. And I can't deny that your willingness to play along with my charade helped cover up my little trip out on the sound. So…thank you.'' She stood and stacked both their empty plates, carrying them to the sink. ''It's been nice seeing you again.''

He stood, as well. ''It's good to see you, too.''

Busying herself at the sink, she spoke with her back to him. ''I have to get down to the marina. You can let yourself out when you're ready to leave. Just lock the door behind you.''

''May I see you again?''

She turned to face him and there was a remote quality in her sad eyes that told him the answer before she opened her mouth. "No," she said. "That wouldn't be a good idea." She laid the dish towel out to dry and walked to the door, then turned back to him one more time. "Thank you."

He stood in the kitchen as she let herself out and walked down the crushed-shell path. It might not be a good idea in her mind, but as far as he was concerned, it was a great one. She wasn't indifferent to him, he was positive. There was nothing specific he could put his finger on, just a quickening feeling in his gut and the way her eyes danced around, never quite meeting his. She'd been exceedingly careful not to touch him after she'd woken up sprawled all over him, too.

As he locked her door and walked down the path after cleaning up her kitchen, Reese was whistling. He had a kayak to rent.

Three

It was midafternoon and Celia was heartily sick of paperwork. Soon she'd be wishing for something to keep her busy during the long winter days when there were far fewer customers, but right now the big fish were running. Which meant that she was up to her ears in equipment rentals, slip requests, repairs, guided fishing expeditions and whale watches, not to mention novice fishermen who expected to land a fifteen-foot shark on a lightweight line off the end of the pier.

She picked up her mug of tea and took a big gulp, grimacing at the cold beverage. Heavy footsteps outside the shack alerted her that someone was about to enter.

"Hey, there." Reese stood in the doorway, grinning at her.

She set down her mug so hard, tea sloshed perilously close to the rim. "Hello."

"Did you forget about the sea oats?"

She sighed as the morning's telephone call returned. "It was marsh grass. Although some sea oats would be nice, too. And no, I didn't forget. Well, not exactly." Then she raised her eyebrows, wondering what possible interest he could have in sea oats. "Why?"

"I rented a kayak. If you'd like to take a break, we could go now."

"We?" She made the tone deliberately dubious.

But Reese only grinned wider, his dimples carving deep grooves in both cheeks. "I thought you might enjoy some company."

"No, thanks." She shrugged. "I'm used to going alone."

"Being used to it and enjoying it are two different things. Besides, it would go faster if you had help."

She was growing annoyed. He wouldn't take a reasonably polite refusal, so she supposed she was off the hook if she got rude. "Reese, I thought I made it clear this morning that I didn't want to reestablish a...friendship with you. It's been thirteen years—"

"And one month and five days."

She stopped, dumbfounded. "You're making that up."

"Nope. Last time I ever saw you was on August the twenty-seventh. It's the second of October." His face grew sober. "I guess I can't blame you for not wanting to renew our friendship. I just thought..." He stopped. "Never mind." He turned away from the door.

"You thought what?" The words were impulsive.

She couldn't believe he knew to the day when he'd left. As much as she'd thought of him over the years, she hadn't even known that. She'd been so miserable when he'd left her behind that her memories of that time had simply blurred.

He paused, his back to her, and his shoulders rose and fell. "I've been away from home for a long time. I cut my ties when I left, family, friends, everything. It just was…really, really *nice* to be with someone who shared my past."

There was a heavy moment of silence in the wake of the words, and her heart filled with pity. The very fact that he knew to the day how long it had been since he'd left had far more to do with the estrangement from his family than it did her, she was sure. She was on her feet and across the small office before she even realized what she was doing. "I'm sorry, Reese. I guess I'm too touchy." She put one hand on his forearm. "I know how it feels to be alone."

He wore a short-sleeved T-shirt with a yacht manufacturer's logo on it and, beneath her fingers, his skin felt hot, rough with whorls of heavy masculine hair, the tendons and muscles tough and hard and tense. The sensations made her acutely aware of how tall and powerful he was, how feminine and needy he made her feel. She knew it was stupid to spend any more time in his company. He could upset the carefully balanced emotions she'd worked so hard to manage in the past two years and leave.

And leave. That was exactly right. And then he'd leave. If she could remember that, and treat this as a temporary visit from an old friend who wouldn't be staying long, surely she could manage it.

Reese hadn't moved. Finally he nodded his head

her way. "I'm sorry if I've made you uncomfort-able." He turned and looked her in the eye, his gaze warm and full of unmistakable affection. From the memories they shared? "It was good to see you again, Celia. Really good." Briefly he lifted his free hand and clasped it over hers where it still rested on his arm. Then he put his hand out and opened the door, stepping away from her.

"No! Reese, wait. I'd like to go kayaking with you." She followed him through the door. "In fact, I'd appreciate the company. I spend too much of my time alone."

He froze in midstride, then slowly turned back to her, eyes cautious. "Sure?"

She took a deep breath, then met his eyes and nod-ded. "I'm sure." She indicated her office. "Just let me get this stuff organized and tell Angie I'm leav-ing."

Twenty minutes later they'd donned jackets against the light breeze and soon were stroking through the water in smooth unison. She set the pace while Reese sat behind her and it gave her a funny feeling to see the flash of his paddle synchronized perfectly with hers. It was ridiculous to interpret the action as inti-macy, and yet that was exactly how it felt. She was left awkward and tongue-tied.

"It's still a lot like I remember." Reese's voice startled her as they paddled out of the harbor and around a corner of the Lower Cape shoreline.

"In the off season, it is," she agreed, relieved by the ordinariness of the topic. "But in the summer, the crowds are horrific. Seems like there are twice as many tourists as there were when I was a kid."

"It's that way in Florida, too."

"Florida?"

"That's where I live now."

"Ah." She couldn't prevent a small burst of laughter.

"What's so funny?"

She shrugged. "I guess I assumed you were still a drifter, sailing from one place to another."

He laughed, too. "Thirteen years would be a long time to drift."

"I guess it would, but that's always how I thought of you. Sailing around the world, seeing new places just like you always said you wanted to."

"You thought of me?"

She could have hit herself over the head with her paddle. "You know, just in passing."

"I thought of you," he said softly.

She didn't know what to say. Finally she said, "I suppose it's only natural that each of us has wondered about the other from time to time."

Now Reese was the one who was silent.

They paddled along, skirting the broken coastline and the many little inlets along it. Seagulls checked them out to see if there was any chance of scrounging a meal, and they passed a tidal flat where two young girls in overalls squelched in the mud, raking half-heartedly for quahogs.

"I did it, you know." He broke the quiet.

"Did what?"

"Sailed around the world."

"I never doubted it." That was the truth. "Tell me about it." Even she could hear the wistful quality in her voice. She'd always said she wanted to leave the Cape and see the world. There'd been a time when she'd assumed she'd be doing it with him.

"I headed south and down through the Caribbean. Stopped for a week here, a few days there. My favorite island was St. John in the Virgins. Extraordinary scenery and at that time still mostly undeveloped. Then I came north on the west side of the Florida coast, went across the Gulf, down around South America and up the other side to the Pacific—"

"That must have taken a while."

"I wasn't in any rush."

Translation: he'd had nowhere to be, nobody to whom he'd needed to report. "Were you alone?"

"Yeah. I had a small cruiser that I could handle myself. But I met a guy in Hawaii who started crewing for me and we headed across the Pacific." The timbre of Reese's voice reflected fondness. "He stayed with me the rest of the trip. Remind me to tell you sometime about the hurricane we weathered."

"My God, Reese!" Her heart shot into her throat, despite the fact that he was sitting right behind her, alive and well. "What possessed you? You could have been killed."

"Don't think that didn't occur to us about two hundred times," he said dryly. "Let's just say that I have no desire to repeat the experience."

"I should think not." Then she gestured toward the shore. "Let's head into that thicket. I gather grass there a lot. It's got a good variety of stuff."

"Isn't it protected?"

"I've got a permit," she said smugly. "Local economy, and all that."

"All right." Reese dug his paddle into the water and turned the kayak efficiently. "The lady's wish is mine to grant."

As they moved into the shallower waters and followed a stream that wound among the shrubby bushes and long-stemmed marsh plants, Celia lifted her face to the autumn sun and said, "I love this time of year. And it's so peaceful out here. I can't remember the last time I did this."

"When you gathered grasses for wreaths?" Reese suggested.

She shook her head. "I paid one of the neighbor kids to come get them for me last time. Too busy."

"You spend a lot of time at the marina?"

She nodded, shifting so that she could look at him. "It's a full-time job."

"Did you work there when your husband was harbormaster?"

It was touchy ground and she could tell from the regretful look on his face that he recognized it the minute he'd said it. "I didn't work."

"You were a full-time mother."

It didn't hurt quite as intensely as she expected and she actually felt her face relax into a soft smile as an image of Leo's little head bent intently over his building blocks flitted through her mind. "Yes."

"Why did you take over after your husband passed away?"

She shrugged. "I knew how to do it. Before we were married I worked for his father. That's how we met. And after we were married, I still helped out sometimes until Leo was born." She paused. It was the first time she could remember that she'd been able to speak of her son without falling apart. "I didn't go to college so my options were pretty limited."

"Wasn't there life insurance?"

The question startled her. "Wha— Oh, yes." Then she realized he thought she needed the money. "Actually, Milo left me in good financial shape," she told him. "I just didn't want to sit around the house all day."

"Too lonely." Unspoken between them was the knowledge that her husband hadn't been all that was lost.

"Yes." She was glad her voice was steady. She concentrated on using the sickle she'd brought along to cut wide swaths of some of the prettier stands of grass. Autumn was a good time to gather it. While she used more supple, still-green flora in wreaths, she also dried bunches of grasses for the standing arrangements she donated to several local charity efforts throughout the year.

After a few moments the quiet work began to soothe her. Reese seemed to anticipate her every move because he maneuvered the kayak around so carefully that she was rarely out of reach of the plants she was seeking. He was right—it did go much faster with his help.

"Look." His low whisper caught her attention. "What is that?"

She scanned the direction he was pointing, finally finding the speckled bird neatly camouflaged among the greens, grays and browns of the marsh grasses. "It's a duck. A gadwall, to be exact. Aren't they pretty?"

"Very. Different from most of the ducks I'm familiar with. Isn't it a little late to be hanging around here?"

"The ducks don't migrate," she told him. "Most of the local varieties stay here all winter long. It's when they find their mates." Good grief. Could she have said anything more awkward?

But Reese didn't leap onto her unintended innuendo as she'd feared. "I never spent a winter out here. Our place was strictly a summer residence."

"It's open now."

Reese's gaze shot to hers. "It is?"

She shrugged, not wanting him to think she kept tabs on members of his family. "I heard in town that one of your brothers was going to be there for a week or so with his family."

"Which brother?" His lips twisted in a smile that was more bittersweet than amused. "I didn't even know any of them had gotten married."

"I believe it was Nicholas." She knew exactly who it was.

"Nick's married?" He was completely still, and she could see the regret in his face. "He wrote to me after I left. I got letters from him for a couple of years."

"You lost touch?"

"I never got *back* in touch," he corrected her.

She was shocked. "At all?"

He shook his head.

He'd mentioned cutting ties, but… "Are you telling me you haven't had *any* contact with anyone in your family since you left?"

He nodded again, his expression unreadable. "Right."

Impulsively she said, "Why don't you give your brother a call? I'm sure your family has missed you as much as you've missed them."

His face was set. "I'll think about it."

Sure he would. "Please," she said, "consider it, Reese. You'll be sorry for the rest of your life if you don't take the chance while you still can."

"I said I'd think about it," he said irritably. Then he made an effort to smile. "Sorry. Coming back here has me thinking about all kinds of things I haven't let myself think of in years."

The silence hummed with unspoken words and she turned back to her task, supremely uncomfortable again. She knew exactly what he meant.

They didn't address anything of consequence for the rest of the trip and returned to the marina shortly before six. She ran home and brought her car down to the marina to load the grasses into the trunk while Reese waited. A part of her wanted to dismiss him and to get far, far away from Reese Barone before she did something stupid, but an equally insistent part of her lobbied for more contact.

"Would it go faster if I helped?" he asked as they brought the newly harvested materials into the workroom she'd converted in the adjacent shed. "I've never made wreaths before but I'm game to try."

She had to smile at the image of the rugged outdoorsman working at the delicate craft. As she smiled she said, "I don't know if you'll want to once you see what it takes, but at the least, I should feed you to thank you for your help."

His gaze caught and held hers and she found that she couldn't take a deep breath for the butterfly wings that crowded into her stomach. "That would be nice."

As they turned and walked toward the kitchen door, he caught her hand in his, threading his fingers through hers. Neither of them spoke. When they reached the door, he let her hand slide free as naturally as if they held hands every day.

But as she assembled a salad and started defrosting

some spaghetti sauce she'd made a few weeks earlier, she realized she was trembling. What was she going to do about Reese Barone?

In the end she did nothing. After the meal he helped with cleanup before they returned to the shed. She showed him how much wire she needed to fasten the wreaths together and he cut it while she worked the grapevine into sizable wreaths that she then began to decorate with a variety of materials.

When she'd finished the raffia bow on the last wreath, she turned to him with a relieved smile. "Thank you for taking me to the marsh today. It was fun."

"How long has it been since you let yourself do something just for fun?" His eyes were serious.

Her hands stilled on the extra grapevine she was coiling. "I don't know. A while."

"How long is a while?"

She concentrated, but she honestly couldn't come up with an answer. She gestured helplessly. "I can't remember."

"That's what I thought."

"But today was lovely."

"It was," he agreed, "but it wasn't solely dedicated to the pursuit of fun. You need to give yourself permission to relax and enjoy life again, Celia."

Instantly she felt her eyes fill with tears. Oh, damn. "Maybe I don't want to. I feel guilty, Reese. Can you understand that?"

"Not like you can. But I know what you mean." He laid down the wire cutters he'd been about to put away and came around the table. When he reached out and took her by the elbows, she let him pull her against him but she kept her head down, stubbornly gazing at the buttons on his knit shirt. "My best friend, Kent—the guy I mentioned earlier—and his wife were killed in an accident at sea a few years ago. Every once in a while I feel absolutely awful for living and laughing and just being happy when they no longer can."

"Oh, Reese, I'm so sorry." She put her arms around his broad back and hugged him closer. "Life hasn't been terrific for either one of us, has it?"

"No." He brushed a stray tendril of hair back from her face with a gentle hand. "But it's getting better again." His gaze locked with hers and for one long, intense moment, his eyes remained unguarded. In them she saw regret, longing, tenderness, desire…and she tore her gaze away, unable to sustain the intimate exchange.

"Celia." The word was a rough whisper of sound. One long finger, calloused from hours of sailing, slipped beneath her chin and lifted it. His dark head came down, blotting out the light, and she closed her eyes automatically as his lips slid onto hers.

Her whole body leaped in delighted response as his mouth settled firmly over hers, molding and shaping. *Yes!* it shouted. Without giving herself time to think about the foolishness of kissing Reese Barone, she sank against him with a soft hum of pleasure, her hands sliding up to the back of his neck and stroking through his thick, warm hair.

Reese's arms tightened. His mouth grew demanding, and she parted her lips to allow him inside as one large hand slid down her back to press her body against his. He was hard and hot and utterly male, making her feel feminine and fragile and surprisingly vulnerable, though it wasn't an unpleasant sensation.

She hadn't been held by a man since Milo died. Dear heaven, she'd forgotten how good it could be.

It was never this good with anyone but Reese.

"Spend the day with me tomorrow." It was a command.

She hung in his arms, clutching his heavy biceps, unable to process the words.

"Say yes," he said, and his voice was urgent.

"Yes," she repeated obediently.

"Good!" He claimed her mouth again before she could take back the word, then quickly released her and stepped away. "I would stay longer, but I'm not sure I'd be able to make myself leave," he said frankly, "and you're not ready for anything more."

And before her befuddled brain could formulate a response, he sketched her a quick salute and headed out the door. "I'll be here at ten."

The phone rang as Celia was getting ready to meet Reese in the morning.

It was Roma, and she was bubbling over with questions. "I called you yesterday afternoon but Angie said you'd gone out on the water with Reese Barone."

"Yes." She knew Roma would have a fit if she didn't explain, and she couldn't resist teasing her a little.

"And...?"

"He helped me gather some stuff for my wreaths."

"And...?"

"The weather was beautiful."

"Celia!"

She chuckled. "Did anyone ever tell you you're nosy?"

"Yes. What happened?" It was hard to insult someone who freely acknowledged her failings.

"Nothing happened." *At least, not while we were out on the water.*

"Why'd he come back?"

"I don't know. His family does have a home here, remember?"

"That didn't seem to matter to him before." A pause. "Is he still the same as you remember?"

"More or less. It's been…nice to talk to him again."

"Oh, come on, Ceel. I bet it's been more than 'nice.' Angie says he's still a total hottie."

"He's not bad."

"So…do you still have feelings for him?"

"That was thirteen years ago, Roma. I married another man, remember?"

"So you do." Roma cut right through any attempt to distract her.

Celia sighed. "I have wonderful memories of my first love. Seeing Reese brings back a lot of those memories. But it doesn't mean anything more than that."

"Right." Roma's voice was dry.

"It doesn't!" She was getting a little annoyed and it showed in her voice.

"Sorry." But Roma didn't sound sorry. "But I've known you long enough to know when you're fibbing. What if Reese came back to find you after all these years? Would you still be interested?"

"He didn't, so it's a moot point. But no, of course not. I moved on and I imagine he did, too."

"Maybe." Roma didn't sound convinced. "But I

still think it's odd that he'd show up here out of the blue. Angie says he's alone and he's not wearing a wedding ring.''

She was going to have to talk to Angie about encouraging these fantasies of Roma's. "I didn't check." That much was true. It had never occurred to her that Reese might be married.

"Well, if he's not, then there's no reason you two couldn't get back together."

"I am not interested in getting married again."

"Who said anything about getting married?" Her best friend's voice was relentlessly cheerful and supremely innocent. "A steamy fling might be a good thing for you. And who better to scratch your itch than a guy you already know you're compatible with in that way?"

"Are you nuts?" Celia demanded. "I do *not* need any itches scratched."

"All right." Roma sighed gustily. "Just trying to help." Her voice grew gentle. "It's okay to go on living, honey."

"I know." She was abruptly perilously close to tears. "But jumping into bed with an old flame just because it might be fun isn't my style." She glanced at the clock above the sink in her kitchen. "I have to go. I'll talk to you next week." No way was she telling Roma she'd kissed Reese last night, or that she was spending time with him today. She already knew she should have her head examined.

After ending the conversation, she dressed quickly and went down to the marina. If she was going to take time off, she needed to check in at the office to make sure everyone had their instructions for the day.

* * *

An hour later Reese stuck his head into her office. "Hey."

"Hey." She looked up from her computer and smiled. Then the smiled faded as she remembered the way they'd parted last night, and a ridiculous shyness spread through her.

Reese stepped inside and closed the door behind him. As he started across the office, he held her gaze and her heart leaped into her throat. She rose from her chair. "What's wrong?"

"Nothing." His voice was husky, his eyes serious. "I figured that if we don't get this out of the way first, we'll both be wondering about it all day."

"What?"

"This." His hand curled around the back of her neck and tugged her toward him as his head came down. He kissed her sweetly, lingering over her mouth and finally drawing back with a bemused smile. "I used to try to convince myself that it really hadn't been that great between us, that you were so unforgettable only because we'd split up while things were still fantastic." His brushed his lips over hers one more time. "I was wrong."

She didn't know what to say. It seemed disloyal to admit how often she'd thought of him. She could barely admit that to herself. But she couldn't resist lifting her hand and briefly cradling his lean cheek in her palm. He closed his eyes and tilted his head into her hand.

And then the door opened.

They leaped apart like two teenagers caught parking by a cop.

"Oops!" Angie's voice was merry. "Sorry, boss.

I just need the invoice for that bluefish charter to-day.''

"Not a problem." Celia was proud that her voice was steady. She turned back to her desk, found the piece of paper, then handed it over to Angie. "So you have everything under control?"

"No problem." Angie smiled at Reese. "Get her out of here. She never takes a break."

Four

To Celia's surprise, Reese asked if she'd like to go to the arts festival over on Nantucket. When she agreed, he led her down to his slip and they boarded the *Amalie*.

She couldn't help wondering about the unusual name. Who was Amalie? Had she been a woman important to Reese in the thirteen years he'd been away?

She wasn't about to betray how unsettled she felt at the thought. It was ridiculous—and totally naive—to expect that he hadn't had some serious relationships. Her stomach did a funny little dance. He even could have been married. Reese, married to someone else. True, she'd married someone else, but... She could hardly acknowledge the rush of wicked jealousy she felt at the mere idea of Reese and another woman.

Was it possible that he felt the same way, thinking

of Milo? If he did, he certainly hid it well. Even the night she'd told him about her family, he'd been nothing but kind and sympathetic. He'd shown absolutely no trace of the foaming-at-the-mouth fury she could feel if she allowed herself to think about it much more.

And she suddenly felt very deflated. Of course he hadn't been jealous. Reese had moved on years ago. He'd proven it when he'd left her behind.

"Celia?" Reese took her hand. "Watch your step." He stopped her just before she would have tripped over someone's deep-sea fishing equipment spread out all over the dock as they cleaned the decks.

Summoning a smile she said, "Thanks." She couldn't meet his eyes, though, and she was thankful for the bright sunlight that had demanded she wear her sunglasses.

Before casting off for Nantucket, Reese gave her a quick tour of his boat, a design less than a year old with every conceivable amenity. The interior was warm, rich mahogany with lighter accents. There was a large-screen television, a computer and a navigation system with all the bells and whistles, and three state-rooms, one of which contained an enormous bed covered in a gorgeous ivory comforter.

She went topside fast, not caring if Reese thought she was running away. She was. Being in a room with Reese Barone and a big bed was a bad, bad idea.

They made the short trip across the sound to the old whaling town. Walking away from the wharf, Celia felt as if every resident on the Cape was there, staring at the Widow Papaleo and her new companion. It was all in her head, she was sure, because locals rarely attended these things. They were strictly for the tourists and had supplanted the sea as the mainstay of the whole Cape's economy, but still, there was no denying she felt odd. Intellectually she knew what it was. People expected certain things of those who were grieving. And even though it had been more than two years, she was afraid they would be critical if they saw her with another man. Why wouldn't they? She was critical of herself!

She wondered if she would harbor the same guilty-pleasure kind of feeling if her companion was a new acquaintance, someone with whom she hadn't shared such a complicated—and intimate—past. Maybe that was it. She felt as if everyone walking by knew exactly what she and Reese had been up to on all those boating expeditions years ago.

But Reese didn't appear to entertain any of the same concerns. He took her to a lobster bar for lunch and they dined on a rooftop deck beneath a sun umbrella. It might be October, but the whole year had been unseasonably warm and dry and it was still pleasant during the day. After lunch they wandered the terraced cobblestone streets and eventually headed down to Old North Wharf where they perused the work of the many local artists who immortalized Nantucket's charm.

"I like this guy's work," Reese said, stopping before one easel. "The view of the town from the harbor is a nice perspective."

Celia chuckled. "Guess you didn't see the painting hanging above the sideboard in my dining room. It was done by him."

But Reese wasn't listening anymore. His attention was riveted on the window of a small pub that fronted the street.

Celia followed his gaze, trying to discern what had distracted him. All she saw were families and couples enjoying late-afternoon cocktails and snacks. One couple, in particular, looked as if they were enjoying each other a lot more than their drinks, and she winced as the man dragged the woman close and devoured her mouth in a sloppy display of far-too-public lust.

When she glanced back at Reese, his expression mirrored her own.

She couldn't help smiling. "Don't care for PDAs?"

"PDAs?" He was still watching the couple.

"Teen slang for Public Display of Affection. Hiring so many kids keeps me up on high-school-speak."

"Mmm."

"Reese? Is something wrong?" He was still focused on the couple.

"That man," he said, "is my cousin Derrick."

"Your cousin!" She was torn between happiness for him that he might get to talk with a family member and dismay that the man appeared so oblivious to appropriate public behavior. "Maybe he's had a bit too much to drink. He seems a little…unaware of his surroundings."

"I doubt it." Reese's voice was surprisingly cool. "Derrick will do just about anything for attention."

"He's certainly getting it now." Around the couple, people were casting covert, scandalized glances as hands strayed and mouths wandered. One couple got up, took their young children firmly by the hand and left a nearby table with a scathing comment. Reese's cousin looked after them and Celia was slightly shocked when he laughed. He had to be close to Reese's age and yet he was acting like a hormone-driven teenage boy.

Reese was shaking his head. "Derrick's point of view has always been a little off kilter."

"Off kilter? Like how, exactly?"

Reese shrugged. "He had what I can only call a mean streak. We all learned not to tell him about things that mattered to us or he'd ruin them and laugh about it. In fact," he said as he looked again at the couple, "I could almost swear that woman with him is Racine Madison. She was his brother's girlfriend all through high school. I can see Derrick wanting her just because she was Daniel's once upon a time."

"She's not Racine Madison anymore," Celia informed him. "Her last name is Harrow now, and she's married to the junior senator from New York."

Reese's eyebrows rose and he whistled. "Derrick hasn't changed, then. He's just graduated from coveting other guys' girlfriends to having affairs with other men's wives." His face wore an expression of resignation. "Amazing. I'm gone all these years and I come home to find at least one thing completely unchanged."

"What do you mean?"

"Derrick has a twin, Daniel, who's the nicest guy you'll ever meet. He's also good-looking, smart, popular and excellent at sports. Derrick, I think, spent most of his childhood feeling like he ran a poor second. He was always trying to get attention any way he could. The older he got, the more obnoxious he got." He shook his head. "His brother and his sisters are great people, so it can't have been his upbringing. He certainly wasn't lacking for money, he's decent-looking enough, and he's got more smarts than most of the rest of us put together. And yet he spent our growing-up years looking for ways to cause trouble.''

''Some people are just like that,'' she said. ''There may not be a reason, except for one that didn't really exist outside his own imagination.''

Reese nodded and she saw a touch of sadness in his eyes. ''I think he never believed that anyone could accept him for who he was.''

''Would you like to go speak to him?'' After all, this was a member of Reese's family whom he hadn't seen in years, albeit not his favorite one.

''No,'' he said decisively. ''This sounds harsh, but Derrick is probably the one person I *haven't* missed. Today is our day. Come on.'' He reached for her hand and threaded her fingers through his, tugging her along the wharf in the opposite direction.

Celia followed automatically, awash in the sensations and feelings produced by the simple clasp of their hands. He'd held her hand just like this years ago. In fact, they'd rarely walked anywhere that he hadn't been touching her in some small way. It had made her feel safe and secure, half of a whole. It was only now that she realized how incomplete her life had been after he left. No wonder she'd walked around in a fog. He'd been her anchor, her strength, her reason to get up in the morning.

And then he'd left. For a while she'd been too depressed to care about anything. But gradually she'd realized that life would go on and, if she was going to survive, that she'd better depend on herself rather than soak up some man's reflected strength.

And she had. Even when she'd married Milo, she'd never let him mean as much to her as Reese once had. Tears stung her eyes as a whole new barrage of guilt assaulted her. She hadn't been as good a wife as she knew she could have been, because she'd been so determined to protect her heart that she'd never let Milo beyond a certain point. Telling herself that he'd never known anything was wrong was little consolation.

She tugged at the grip of Reese's hand, trying to slide her fingers free. But Reese only tightened his grip. "What's the matter?"

"I don't want the whole Cape buzzing about me holding a strange man's hand," she said. "Could you please let go?"

But he ignored her. "Don't you like it?"

Well. She couldn't say no, because she *did,* far too much. But she couldn't say yes or he'd be smug for the rest of the day. Besides, admitting it would give him far too much power over her. "That's beside the point."

"So you do like it. Good. So do I." He lifted their joined hands and brushed a kiss across her knuckles. "I never let myself think about how much I missed you until I saw you again."

She closed her eyes against the serious intensity of his. It just didn't seem fair, somehow, that he could desert her for so long, and yet the moment he showed up, her body and her emotions were more than ready to take a flying leap back into the middle of a relationship with him. This was only the third day since he'd returned, and already she felt as if they were a couple again.

He still had her hand enclosed in his, and she suspected that arguing with him about it would only be a waste of time. Reese had an instinct for distracting her and he made her arguments seem silly and inconsequential. She might as well save her energy.

Besides, if she were completely honest, she was enjoying every second of the day.

Better not enjoy it too much. He'll leave again and you'll fall flat on your face just like the last time. It was good to remind herself of that. No matter how much she enjoyed his attention and his caresses, he'd be leaving. So whatever she did with him, she had to keep in mind that it was just a temporary thing.

After another hour of strolling the small whaling community, they worked their way to the top of the town, then decided to head back to his boat, docked at Straight Wharf. In a small ice-cream shop on the way, they found Baronessa gelati, the Italian ice cream Reese's grandfather had established in Boston, famous nationwide now.

"Have you kept track of the family business at all?" Celia asked as they sat on a graceful wood-and-iron bench along Upper Main Street, eating their gelati. The day was cooling but still lovely, the reds and yellows of the autumn foliage enhancing the rosy bricks of so many of the historic buildings.

"No. It was never something that interested me much to start with. My mother used to say I was born to be the wild one." His smile was tinged with sadness. "I guess she was right. My older brother, Nick, was the one who liked the whole business angle. We all figured he'd become Mr. Baronessa someday, and he did."

"Yes." She knew that Nicholas Barone was the CEO of the family company now. "But have you heard anything about the fire or the problems the company has had?"

Reese's gaze sharpened. "What fire?"

"Several months ago, in the spring, there was a fire at the manufacturing plant. One of the family members was injured—"

"Who?" His concern was evident.

She shrugged helplessly. "I'm sorry, I can't remember the name. It was a woman."

"Colleen? Gina, Rita, Maria—"

"No. Do you have a sister named Amy, or Annie?" *Amalie.* Maybe that was where the boat's name came from. "I think it was something like that."

"Emily?"

"That was it." Her heart sank. Not Amalie, but Emily.

"She's not my sister, she's my cousin. Derrick, the guy we saw today, is her brother. Was she badly hurt?"

"I don't think so. But the last I heard, the investigators were calling it 'suspicious in origin.'"

"Meaning arson."

"Yes."

"Arson," he repeated. "Who would want to burn down our plant?"

She wondered if he even realized he still thought of himself as a member of the Barone family. "I can't imagine. Does Baronessa have rivals?"

He snorted. "Every company has rivals. But there's a big difference between competition and burning down a rival's business."

"What about someone who's angry at someone in your family? Some kind of grudge, maybe."

His eyebrows rose, and his eyes were focused on a distant past as he answered her. "Our family has had a sort of feud going on for years now with another

Sicilian family who owns a restaurant called Antonio's. But that feud involved my grandfather, and I can hardly imagine it carrying over into our generation. Besides, it's impossible to imagine the Contis sanctioning arson.''

They finished their gelati in silence, then walked back to Reese's boat and headed home to the Cape.

As they skimmed across the choppy sound to the marina, she thought, *What a perfect day.* It was too darn bad that Reese was still the most impossibly attractive man she'd ever known. And that he still could light her fire with no more than a look from those silvery eyes she'd always loved so much. It would be all too easy to get used to being with Reese again, and that would be a terrible mistake.

Because she knew from bitter experience that he couldn't be trusted to stay.

When they docked at the marina he could sense that she was eager to be gone. He vaulted over the rail onto the dock before she could scurry off and said, ''Let's get some shrimp for dinner.''

Celia hesitated. ''Reese,'' she said in a strained voice, ''today was very nice. But I don't think—''

''I do.'' He took her hand and started to pull her along the dock before she could refuse him. ''We both have to eat. We might as well eat together.''

''I can't. I already have plans,'' she said, and her voice was sincere. ''I'm sorry. If I'd known you were going to be in town, I'd have postponed.''

Until you were gone. She didn't say it aloud but he suspected she was thinking it.

Well, he had news for her. If she thought he was

going to disappear from her life again, she was dead wrong.

Whoa! Say what?

He took a deep breath. All right. He might as well admit it. He was falling for Celia all over again and he had no intention of leaving this time. At least, not unless she came along.

"Reese? Come back." She was waving a hand in front of his face. "I really am sorry. But there's something I have to do."

"It's all right," he said. "It's not as if we're on a tight schedule." She got a funny look on her face, but before she could pursue his statement, he threaded her fingers through his. "Give me a kiss to keep me going until tomorrow."

Her eyes widened. "Are you crazy? I'm the boss. I'd never live it down if anyone saw us."

He made an exaggerated crestfallen face.

She chuckled. Then, gazing into his eyes, both hands still entwined with his, she pursed her lips and sent him a single, long-distance kiss across the space between them. She was smiling slightly, and it was the craziest thing— Despite the fact that she hadn't moved one inch closer, the moment felt more intimate somehow, than if he'd taken her in his arms. Her eyes were tender with unspoken words and they simply stood for what seemed like a long, long time, holding the eye contact.

He nearly asked her what she was thinking, but words would have marred the moment. Finally he offered her a crooked smile. "I guess that was an acceptable compromise."

Her eyes sparkled. "Good."

"This time." He lifted one hand and pressed a final

kiss to her knuckles as he had earlier in the day. "See you tomorrow."

"See you." She hesitated a moment, then turned with resolute steps and made her way back to the harbormaster's shack.

He had a solitary dinner of fried clams in his tiny mess that evening. Ordinarily he might have gone looking for a little bar where the locals traded fish and tourist tales, but if he couldn't be with Celia, he didn't want to be with anyone.

Yikes. Thoughtfully, he rolled the single can of beer he'd had with dinner back and forth in his palms. Seemed like every time he allowed himself to think, his brain came up with another idea he hadn't consciously let himself consider.

But it was true. He *didn't* want to be with anyone other than Celia. In the thirteen years they'd been apart, he'd met a lot of women, known some of them intimately. Once he'd even let a girlfriend move in briefly, just long enough to realize it was a colossal mistake. He'd never preferred spending any time outside the bedroom with a woman to hanging with his buddies, and he'd certainly never felt that he couldn't live without one.

Until now.

After he cleaned up his dinner, he watched the evening news. By then it was almost dark and he took a second beer, grabbed a sweatshirt and headed topside to sit in a deck chair, prop his feet on the rail and look at the stars. It was peaceful. Most of the other yachts weren't occupied and he practically had the dock to himself.

So what was he going to do about Celia?

"Hey, Reese! How you doing?" A feminine voice broke the silence.

Damn. He really didn't feel like being social this evening. The voice belonged to Claudette Mason, the woman he'd met the night he'd caught Celia sneaking around. He'd seen Claudette a few times since then, working around her employer's boat or walking to and from the market, but he'd made it a point to be brief. The woman was as unsubtle as they came and clearly on the prowl.

"Hey, Claudette. I'm great." He purposely didn't ask her how she was in return. Maybe she'd get the hint.

"Hello, Mr. Barone. I'm Neil Brevery." It was a smooth, unfamiliar masculine voice. "We haven't met but Claudette has mentioned you."

Ah, hell. He rose to his feet and crossed the deck to the side, where he stepped onto the pier and extended his hand. "My pleasure, Neil. Call me Reese."

The man standing before him was easily twenty years older than the curvaceous Claudette, at least half a foot shorter than he was, slight and almost comical in baggy Bermuda shorts and a brightly patterned tropical shirt. Reese wondered exactly what Claudette's job description was; it was difficult to imagine that Brevery had hired her solely for her skills with a boat. "Are you one of the Boston Barones?"

"Actually, I live in Florida." He'd repeated the words many times in response to that very query and found that they usually discouraged further prying. "Just up here visiting an old friend. And you?"

"I have several homes around the world. Strictly in warm locations." Brevery gave a dry chuckle. "I like to visit the northern regions but I could never live here when it gets cold.'' Then he gestured toward his own boat, docked a number of slips away. ''Ernesto Tiello's coming over for a game of poker. Would you care to join us?''

''Oh, yes, please do.'' Claudette was all but purring. So much for the hope that she'd tone down the vamp act in front of her employer.

He really didn't want to spend the evening gambling, which he loathed. And he wanted to spend it even less with a bunch of strangers. ''I'm sorry,'' he said, lying through his teeth unapologetically, ''but I've got plans in just a little while. Perhaps some other time.''

''Most definitely.''

''Yes. We'll be here for at least another two weeks.'' Claudette struck a pose that thrust her considerable assets into prominent view.

''We may,'' Brevery corrected her. ''Then again, I may take a notion to head for another port.'' There was an edge to his voice. ''Come, Claudette. Let's not keep Ernesto waiting.''

''Yes, sir.'' Claudette's eyes lowered. He got the distinct impression she'd received a reprimand, though he couldn't imagine why.

Brevery extended his hand again. ''Nice meeting you, Reese. We'll have to try to set up a card game for another night.''

''Nice meeting you, also.'' *I'll be busy every night I'm here.* He had to stifle the urge to speak the words aloud as Brevery moved on, Claudette sauntering along in his wake.

Damn. Now what was he going to do? He was quite sure there would be some surreptitious checking

going on to see when and if he left his yacht. So much
for his quiet, relaxing evening. Served him right for
lying in the first place. But he wasn't sorry. No way
did he want to spend the evening fending off nosy
neighbors' questions and a pushy female's advances.
He vaulted back onto the deck and picked up his
empty beer can, taking it into the galley and crushing
it in the recycler. There was no help for it. He was
going to have to go *somewhere*.

What the hell. He'd go sit on Celia's porch. Surely
she wouldn't mind. And it wasn't as if she'd be home.
He'd just stay an hour or so and then come back. By
then, he could make excuses about an early night.

With the decision made, he slipped into his dockside shoes and locked the cabin, then left the pier and
hiked through the little town of Harwichport. Many
of the tourist places were dark, but the residents'
homes had light spilling from windows and he caught
the occasional glimpse of a family moving around
inside.

Families. If he'd waited for Celia, or if he'd returned when she was older, would they have had a
chance? Could they have had children of their own
by now, and a home filled with the same cozy scenes
as those he passed? He loved Amalie dearly, but he
was thirty-four years old and just beginning to realize
how much he'd like to have children of his own
someday.

He tried to picture his own kids, but all he could
come up with was a troop of dark-haired children
much like the ones in family snapshots of his siblings
and himself when they were small. A few of them
had gotten coppery highlights from their mother's
brilliant locks, but for the most part they were dark-

haired, wiry kids with wide, gap-toothed smiles and deep tans from their Harwichport summers. Yeah, he'd like to have a few of those.

With Celia. Another revelation. But one he realized he'd subconsciously imagined for years.

He wondered what her son had looked like. There were no pictures on her walls, no photographs lovingly framed and displayed, of either her son or her husband. It was as if she wanted to forget that that period of her life ever existed.

Having glimpsed the anguish she carried in her heart the night she'd broken down and cried herself to sleep in his arms, he felt his throat tighten. He could understand how difficult it would be to live with that loss, much less be reminded of it on a daily basis every time she saw their faces. And who was he to talk? He'd suffered far less and yet there were no pictures of his family around anywhere, either.

Reaching her house, he let himself in through the little garden gate and mounted the single step to the low porch. He took a seat in one of the old captain's chairs she kept beneath a trellis of roses that probably provided welcome shade in the summer. It was quiet and as peaceful as the night had been earlier. There'd already been the first frost so no crickets or night insects stirred the silence. He slouched back in the chair and exhaled a deep, contented breath, feeling vaguely silly. Celia wasn't even home and yet he was comforted just by being near her things, sitting in a spot he imagined she sat in frequently through the summer. He closed his eyes, tilted his head back. This was nice.

Then a soft, scraping sound caught his attention. Someone was opening Celia's front door from the inside. Instantly he was on his feet. Outrage and adrenaline rushed through him. Celia had been through enough in her life; he had no intention of allowing a burglar to destroy the secure little nest she'd made for herself. His muscles tensed as he prepared to launch himself across the porch to take down the black-clad intruder.

And a second later he realized that the "burglar" was Celia.

"What the hell are you doing?" he growled, unaccountably furious at her.

She jumped and squealed in the way only females could do. But she recovered fast. "What do you mean, what am I doing? What are *you* doing hiding on my front porch?"

"I wasn't hiding," he said stiffly. "I thought you weren't home and the marina was too lively, so I came up here to sit on the porch and enjoy the night." He looked more closely at her clothing, noting the black turtleneck sweater, jeans and sneakers and the black watch cap that covered her head, and a suspicion took root. "Exactly what kind of meeting are you going to at…eight-twenty in the evening?"

"That," she said precisely, "is none of your business."

"It is if you're up to what I think you're up to," he said.

Even in the dark he could see her eyes widen with outrage. "I have a date." Her voice was haughty. "And you're making me late."

"Oh, don't mind me." He walked to her side. "I think I'll just tag along and meet this date."

"You will not!"

"Because there is no date, is there?" He took her

arm and shook her lightly. "You're going out on the water to do your amateur spy thing again, aren't you?"

"Yes." Her voice was defiant. "And don't think for a minute you're going to stop me. I'm not a big fan of caveman behavior."

"I wasn't planning to stop you," he said, forcing a mild tone into his voice, although he longed to tie her up and keep her safe. Caveman, indeed. "But I am coming with you."

"Reese...no." She sounded horrified. "What if something happens?"

"I'm going to do my best to see that it doesn't," he assured her. Then, touched by the anxiety he heard in her voice, he smoothed an errant lock of hair back beneath the edge of the cap. "Celia, how do you think I'd feel if something happened to *you* while you were out there alone?" He felt heat creep up his neck. The last thing he wanted to do was to sound pathetic or needy.

"I—I don't know," she muttered, dropping her head. "You left me alone before."

He wanted to shake her. "Yes, I did. Biggest mistake I ever made."

Her head shot up and she stared fully at him for the first time. "What?"

"I'm never leaving you again," he said tightly. What the hell, he'd already opened the lid. He might as well spill the rest.

The words froze in the chilly autumn air. Celia's eyes were wide and dark in the dim light, and her mouth was a round *O* of surprise.

"Well, hell," he finally said. "I guess this isn't the best way to lead into this conversation."

"I guess not." But the antagonism was gone and her tone sounded almost amused. "Are you serious about coming with me?"

He sighed. "If you're serious about going. But I still think it's a lousy idea. You could get hurt if the wrong people realize what you're doing. I can't believe the Feds would ask a civilian to do such a risky thing."

Celia was silent, her gaze dropping away from his again.

"You little…deceiver," he said through his teeth. "You haven't been asked to do this at all, have you?"

"They did ask me to report any suspicious behavior," she said. "How can I report it unless I see it?"

Reese sighed. "All right. If you insist on going, then I'm coming with you. But this is the last time you do anything like this if I have to tie you to your bed every night."

Her gaze flicked to his and then away again and he knew he'd stepped over the invisible line she had drawn between them.

"Sorry," he said. "I don't know why but all I seem to be able to think of when I'm around you is beds."

As he'd hoped, his wry tone lightened the tense moment and she laughed. "Soon we're going to have to start a list of all the things you can't talk about."

He snorted, turning to lead the way down the steps. "It might be easier to list the topics that *aren't* off-limits."

"I'm sorry." She stopped and he turned around. She raised her hands to his chest and the feel of her small, warm palms burned a hole straight through his clothes to brand his skin.

He shivered, wanting nothing more than to drag her onto one of the chairs in the deep shadow of the porch and shove aside clothing until he could sheathe himself deep within her.

"I don't mean to be so difficult," she whispered.

"I know." He took her wrists and pressed a kiss to the fragile inner side of each, ignoring his arousal in favor of the sweet moment. "You just can't help it."

She chuckled, and he was ridiculously pleased when she didn't immediately move away. "Something like that."

Five

But she wasn't laughing three hours later. They'd untied a kayak that she'd moored at a small pier down the street from the marina and slipped out of the harbor, hugging the marshes here and there along the shoreline. They'd seen nothing; no boats, no lights, no suspicious silhouettes of darkened boats, no unusual activity. Nothing. Finally, just before midnight, he talked her into giving up the vigil.

"What makes you think that this drug activity is based at Harwichport?" They were motionless in a stand of scrub and marsh grass, and he spoke close to her ear in a low voice.

"It may not be here. They could be working out of Wychmere, Saquatucket or Allen. But I can't figure out why Milo would have been a target if they weren't worried about him seeing something at our marina."

He nodded, and she knew she had a point. Her husband wouldn't have posed a threat if the drug trafficking had been centered elsewhere. "It could have been simply a revenge thing," he said.

"I've thought about that, too. But it doesn't make sense. Usually revenge is done with a public purpose in mind, to teach someone else a lesson. Unless it's extremely personal, which I doubt this was. Milo never offended anyone in his whole life. Besides, no one else knew Milo had spoken to the FBI."

"That you're aware of."

She was silent for a moment. "True."

They didn't speak again until they got back to the dock and tethered the boat. Walking up the street to her house, he said, "Celia, you don't know who else might be involved in this. You could wind up the same way your husband and son did if the wrong person suspects you're still digging around."

"I know." She stopped on the small porch. "And until recently I didn't even care. But now..." She shook her head, not caring if he saw the tears on her cheeks. "Dammit, Reese, why did you come back here?"

He stepped forward and gathered her into his arms, laying his cheek against her hair, and she savored the moment as she slipped her arms around his waist and clung. "Because," he said, "I couldn't stay away any longer."

Dropping his head, he sought her mouth. The kiss he gave her was tender, rife with deep feeling, healing lonely aches inside her that she'd known since her family had died. Celia clung to him, needing to be cuddled and coddled, needing the warmth of his hard body surrounding and protecting her. It had been so long since she'd felt safe that she'd forgotten how good it was, and she reveled in his gentle touch.

But it wasn't long before his mouth hardened, became more demanding, his tongue plunging into her moist depths in search of her response. And respond she did. She went limp against him, letting his arms support her, letting him pull her so closely against him that he made a deep growling sound in the back of his throat as their bodies fit together.

He bent her backward over one arm, his free hand slipping beneath her black sweater to caress the silky skin at her waist. His fingers were rough and determined, and she shivered helplessly when his hand slid upward, stroking and exploring her torso. His fingers glided over her ribs until he could cup her breast in his palm, his thumb rubbing ceaselessly over her sensitive nipple, and she shivered in his embrace, her arms coming up to clasp his dark head. Each small stroke sent wild arrows of arousal down to center between her legs, and she writhed against him.

He dragged her back to the swing, deep in the shadows, and settled her across his lap without ever breaking the demanding, tongue-tangling kiss they shared. Celia twisted as he tugged up her sweater to bare her breasts in the shadowed darkness, and when he bent his head and took one nipple into the hot cavern of his mouth, she stifled the sound she made against his shoulder.

"Don't hold back." He plucked at the other taut nipple and she squirmed, pressing her legs tightly together to alleviate the throbbing ache centered there. "Don't hold back," he said again. His free hand left her breast and smoothed down her body, gently probing at her navel, spanning her small waist. She felt a slight tug as he freed the fastening of her pants, and then his warm hand was in her panties, splayed across her abdomen, the tips of his fingers brushing back and forth over the tiny curls he found.

Celia's arms clenched around his neck. Her whole body felt supersensitized, her breath coming in shallow gulps. Had it always been this...*intense* with Reese?

Yes. Always.

His mouth suckled harder at her breast and suddenly she felt a shocking nip of strong teeth as he closed them over the sensitive peak. She gasped and he gentled his mouth immediately while at the same instant he slid his middle finger over her feminine mound and deep into the wiry curls. She gasped again and he lifted his head from her breast and claimed her mouth in another intimate kiss, echoed by the finger between her legs probing gently but insistently at her tight folds. "Spread your legs," he urged. She obeyed. Her whole body tightened when she felt him slide one finger deep into her, and her back arched involuntarily as her body clenched around him, pushing him even deeper.

"Celia," he gasped. "I forgot how good you feel." He rotated his finger slightly, grinding the palm of his hand against the throbbing button of need at the top of her opening, and she cried out, dazed by the intense sensations. The sound of her own voice was startling in the deep shadow of the night porch, and for the first time, she fully realized that they were outside, on her front porch, within hearing—and possibly within sight—of anyone who happened by.

"Wait." She struggled in his arms, gripping his wrist tightly. She had no chance of moving his hand from its intimate nest unless he chose to do so, a fact that she was keenly aware of with the vulnerable knowledge only another woman could understand. Reese stilled his hand, although he didn't withdraw.

"It's all right, baby. It's all right."

"No," she said. "It's not." She swallowed painfully, so aroused by the feel of his hand between her legs that she nearly forgot why she'd protested. "I—I'm not ready for this, Reese."

In the darkness she saw the white flash of his teeth. One finger moved, drawing a whimper of need from her. "I beg to differ. And—" he shoved his hips forward against her hip so that she could feel the rock-hard bulge of his arousal "—I sure as hell am."

"No," she whispered again. "I—I want to but…I'm just not ready."

He stilled, and she realized he understood that she meant it. Finally he heaved a sigh. "Okay. Okay, I can wait. I don't want to rush you into anything." Slowly, he withdrew his hand and she closed her eyes tightly as her body jerked involuntarily at the glide of flesh on flesh. His finger left a cool path of moisture behind and even in the dark, she blushed. Then he spoke again. "Can you tell me why? I mean, I've already stayed the night, technically, so if you're worried about your reputation—"

"It's not that. I just…have to think. A few days ago we hadn't seen each other in thirteen years and now here we are, ready to…"

"Yeah. Ready to." There was wry humor in his voice. He carefully refastened her pants and tugged her sweater down into place, then lifted her and set her beside him on the swing, cuddling her in the crook of his elbow. "Where do you see us going with this, Celia?"

She was silent. "That's not a fair question," she said. "I've barely gotten used to the idea that you're back again."

"It hasn't been any longer for me," he pointed out, "and I'm used to it." He took her face between his palms and gently stroked her lips with his thumbs. "I'm willing to leave the past in the past. Are you?"

She hesitated and his hands dropped away. "Or are you still punishing me for taking off all those years ago?" His voice was rough, frustrated, impatient. "I'm not looking for an affair for a few weeks while I'm in town, so if that's all this is going to be to you, tell me now."

"What *are* you looking for?" She swallowed painfully. "I'm not the same girl you used to know, Reese. I don't have a lot to offer anymore."

"You have everything I want." His voice was low, soothing.

"Not if you're looking for a wife and a family," she said bluntly, too agitated to soften the words. "I don't want children. Ever. I just…I couldn't handle that." She stopped, aware that her voice was rising toward hysteria.

He was silent, and her heart felt as if someone had attached lead weights to it. This was it. Now he would leave. She'd told him how she felt so that he wouldn't expect more than she could give…but she couldn't prevent herself from praying that he didn't walk away.

She caught his wrist and rose with him when he would have moved away from her. She knew she could never be what he wanted. It was wrong of her to encourage him, to give him hope and yet...

"Reese?"

He hesitated, but he didn't pull away from her. Finally he turned and touched her cheek with his free hand, then linked his fingers through hers. "I want you, Celia. Just you." He bent and kissed her swiftly, then walked down the path to her gate. "See you tomorrow."

In the morning the first thing she thought of was Reese. Why had she turned him away last night? Was it self-preservation? Or was he right? Was she punishing him?

She worried at the notion the whole way to the marina, but when she entered the office, Angie's expression erased all thoughts of personal matters from her head. "What's wrong?" she asked.

"Hurricane." Angie indicated the small television they kept atop a file cabinet. "The one they thought was going to move northeast off the coast? Well, it's coming in for a visit."

"Oh, no." Her mind raced. "How long do we have till it gets here?"

Angie shrugged. "Maybe the rest of the day. It tore up the Carolina coast and is headed straight for us." She laid a stack of papers on Celia's desk. "Did you have a boat out last night? I found life preservers hanging on the doorknob this morning."

Celia stiffened. "Yes. Reese and I went night fishing." Duh. Hadn't she used that very same excuse on the night she'd run into Reese?

Angie laughed. "Sure, boss. Night fishing." She was grinning as she walked away.

Celia studied the weather pattern as the meteorologist on the screen droned on. The brunt of the hurricane had missed the southern coastline. But Cape Cod stuck out too far. If it continued due north, they were going to get slammed. She'd seen Hurricane Bob do the same thing more than a decade ago, and that hadn't been nearly as powerful a storm as this one was currently.

Quickly she gathered the rest of the staff and began issuing orders. All equipment needed to be put away, including any watercraft small enough to be removed from the water. Bigger ones should be moored on long lines or moved to small harbors with marshes or sand beaches where they could be grounded without causing the damage that would result if they were tossed by waves into large piles of ruined boats at the pier. Anything that could blow away, even heavy deck furniture, should be stored. Flags and banners down, cancel all charters, close the marina. Get out the plywood and start covering all the windows, tape any that don't get boarded up.

Many of the yachts were already gone, others were battening down and their owners were taking rooms in town. Lodging was easy to come by, since the autumn tourists were fleeing, clogging Route 6 up to the Sagamore Bridge where they headed west away from the water or north toward Boston.

Angie helped her remove the important files and compact discs, and take apart the computer. Then they took the whole mess over and set it up at her house, which would be far safer than the office. Her headquarters was commonly known as "the shack" despite its sturdy appearance. It would be exposed to the waves and storm surge and could easily fall apart if the pier should go.

While she was at home, she double-checked the small generator that would keep her freezer and refrigerator going when the power went down as it inevitably would, pulled oil lanterns from storage and filled them, and brought in armloads of firewood. She filled the bathtub and several extra buckets with water, just in case, and checked the batteries in her flashlights.

Then she headed back to the shack to help finish boarding up before she sent everyone home. Reese's boat still sat in its slip, and she allowed herself to wonder where he was and what he would do during the storm. Part of her wanted to invite him to spend the time with her; the other part told her she was crazy, that she was heading for heartbreak.

"Celia." Ernesto Tiello lumbered up the pier toward her, a sleeveless men's undershirt stretched a little too tightly over his bulky body. He was heavily muscled rather than fat, and he reminded her of nothing so much as a Mafia-type don on one of her favorite television shows. She wondered momentarily whether he kept a weight room aboard his boat. The thought made her shake her head. Rich people.

"Hello, Ernesto. Staying with us through the storm?"

He nodded, his dark eyes grim. "Yes. But I have another question. Have you seen Claudette Mason this morning?"

She shook her head. "No. Did Brevery leave?"

Ernesto shook his head. "No. He has decided to stay, as well."

"I imagine Claudette's probably helping him."

''No.'' His accent was thicker than ever. ''Neil has not seen her this morning. He thinks she may simply have quit. But I am concerned. She would have told me if she were planning to leave.''

''I'm sure she's around,'' Celia soothed. ''Why don't you check with the rest of my staff? One of them might know where she got to.''

''Thank you. I shall. And you will let me know if you should find her?''

''Of course.'' She shook her head as Tiello moved along the pier to where some of her staff were working. The poor man was wild about Claudette, but Celia was sure Claudette didn't return the feeling. Maybe she had simply taken off.

Still, she'd seemed quite content acting as a hostess or whatever it was she did for Neil Brevery while she flirted with everything in pants. There didn't seem to be a physical relationship between Claudette and her employer, although Celia had noticed the woman jumped to attention when the small man spoke. The rest of the time, she acted like a cat in heat.

Now, Celia, be nice. Just because she's drooled over Reese a few times is no reason to show your own claws.

''Hey, woman, why are you scowling?''

She jumped, startled out of her thoughts. Reese stood right in front of her. If he only knew! She smiled, then said, ''Never mind. Have you seen Claudette Mason?''

Reese grimaced. ''No, thank God.''

She couldn't prevent the chuckle. ''Been ducking her advances?''

''Been running like a gazelle,'' he countered. ''There's someone else I'd rather advanced on me.''

"Oh?" She cast him a flirtatious glance, then caught herself. Lord, she was as bad as Claudette.

"Are you going to invite me to weather the storm with you?" He stepped a pace closer and his eyes grew heavy with sensual intent.

"I hadn't thought about it," she lied. "Can't find a room in town?"

He shook his head. "No. It's terrible. Everything's booked solid. Even the emergency shelter at the high school is full. One guy offered me his stable, but I'm too big to sleep in a manger, so…"

She was laughing. "Con artist. I suppose you can come over. Let me finish getting everything stowed here and we'll go." She indicated the television. "From the look of things, this storm is moving a lot faster than they expected. We're not going to have hours to sit around and wait for it."

And they didn't.

He arrived home with her around four, bringing a duffel bag of clothing with him. She felt a little funny marching through the streets with a man carrying what amounted to a suitcase, but she told herself that with the storm coming, everyone would be too busy to wonder about it.

At her house, he nailed the gate shut, took down the porch swing and put away the chairs in her shed, then helped her in the kitchen as she made several dishes that could be eaten cold over the next few days.

The wind had already picked up by seven, and they checked the forecast as a meteorologist pointed out the eye of the enormous storm system moving straight toward them.

They snuggled on the sofa watching the Weather

Channel, which had devoted itself almost exclusively to coverage of the storm. She'd felt both exhilarated and awkward when he'd first put his arm around her, but when he'd made no further moves she relaxed. Now she leaned into his big, warm body with pleasure. He didn't appear to be angry about last night, and for the first time she allowed herself to wonder, just for a moment, whether they had any chance at a future together. Then he spoke and she abandoned her thoughts with relief.

"This could be bad. I guess you've been through your share of wicked storms."

Celia nodded, trying to ignore the erotic sensation of his breath feathering her ear. "A few. But a lot of times, the hype is worse than the actual event. And most of the worst ones were nor'easters. We don't get slammed by hurricanes as often as the southern states do. How about you? Were you living in Florida when Andrew came through?"

Reese shook his head. "No. And my home isn't anywhere close to where the worst of the damage was done. But hurricanes can be killers. I learned that the hard way."

"What do you mean?"

A shadow passed over his features. "Nobody ever thinks bad things can happen to *them*. I told you about my friends Kent and Julie, but I didn't tell you how they died. They took their boat down to the Bahamas for a couple of days. They had a baby at home and hadn't had much time together, and Kent wasn't too worried that there was a hurricane coming. He was a good sailor. He figured if he kept an eye on the forecasts and got out in time, they'd be heading north-west, away from a storm so they'd beat it to the main-land.''

Celia felt a clutch in her stomach as he continued, his face grim and stony.

"But the storm changed course and caught them. I was in radio contact with them for five hours and then…nothing.''

"Oh, Reese.'' She turned in his arms and circled his shoulders. "I'm so sorry.''

"The coast guard never found them, although a few pieces of their boat did eventually wash up.'' He dropped his head to rest against hers.

Poor Reese. He'd lost his family—through circum-stances she still didn't entirely understand—then he'd found a friend—and lost him, too. She didn't speak, sensing that words would be superfluous. The comfort he needed from her superceded oral communication. So she simply pulled him more closely to her and rubbed small circles over his back.

"Celia?''

"Yes?'' She pressed a kiss to his jaw.

"There's something else I'd like to tell you about Kent and Julie—'' But his voice was interrupted by a loud banging at the back door. They both jolted.

"Who in the world is that?'' It had already begun to rain and the wind had picked up significantly, al-though she doubted the winds were gale force. Wrenching open the door, she held it tightly to pre-vent the wind from ripping it out of her hands. "Roma!'' Her friend was drenched, her fine black hair plastered to her head despite the raincoat hood she had over it. "What's wrong?''

"Greg fell off the ladder.'' Her friend's voice

caught. "I hate to impose, but do you have time to help me finish the windows?"

"Of course!" She turned to call to Reese but he was standing right behind her.

"We'll both come," he said. "Have you taken him to the medical center?"

"My father did. Mom's keeping the kids."

"How bad do you think he is?" Celia was already reaching for her raincoat on a hook in the mudroom.

"He's going to need stitches, I think." She made a gesture toward her eye. "He cut his eyebrow open pretty deep."

Celia winced. "Bet he'll have a shiner."

They covered the block and a half to the Lewises' home in short order, and despite the increase in wind and rain, they were able to help Roma nail plywood over her larger windows and put asterisk-shaped crosses of gray electrical tape over the remaining ones.

Just as they were finishing, Roma's father and Greg returned. Rather than stitches, the cut in his eyebrow was covered by a shiny clear coat of something that resembled nail polish. Roma's father explained that it was a special skin sealant—a type of superglue for humans—that wouldn't leave as much of a scar as stitches might.

"I made clam chowder," Roma told them in a half shout over the rising roar of the wind. "Come on in and have some. The least I can do is feed you after working you like that in the middle of this storm."

"Oh, that's all right—"

"Thanks. We'd love to." Reese cut in right over Celia's attempt to wriggle out of the offer.

"Great." Roma turned and headed for the door.

"We'll hang your coats by the woodstove so at least they'll dry a little before you go out again."

As they followed her into the house, Celia cast Reese a dark glance. "Why did you do that?"

"I thought it would be nice to get to know your friends," he told her quietly. "Unless there's some reason you'd prefer I didn't."

"No," she said. "It's not that…"

"Then what?"

But Roma's voice saved her from a reply. "Come on, you two. It's getting nastier out there by the minute!"

They weren't in the house ten minutes when he realized why Celia had been reluctant to stay for dinner. He'd thought—feared—that perhaps she didn't want anyone to see them together. But it wasn't him at all.

Greg and Roma Lewis had three small children. The oldest couldn't have been more than six, and they plainly adored Celia. An older woman he assumed was Roma's mother was feeding a baby girl when they walked in, and the infant squawked and reached for Celia with a wide grin that displayed four teeth and an astonishing amount of drool.

"I know, I know," the woman said, her voice amused. "Gramma can't compete with Aunt Celia. Here." She handed the spoon to Celia. "Would you like to finish the job?"

"I'd love to." Celia took a seat and began feeding the baby, and Reese watched in fascination as she coaxed the little mouth open by repeating a ditty about a choo-choo train entering a tunnel, complete with the *whoo-whoo* of a whistle. This was a side of her he'd never seen and for the first time he could finally envision her as a mother.

Roma introduced him to her parents and her husband, Greg, who shook his hand before wincing and settling into a rocking chair with an ice pack pressed against his head. "Thanks for helping Roma finish up," he said. "I don't know how the hell that happened. One minute I was on the ladder, the next I was eating dirt."

The smaller of the two boys wandered over and surveyed his father with a puckered brow. "Daddy have a boo-boo?"

Greg nodded. "A big boo-boo. But I bet it would feel a lot better if someone kissed it."

"Me, me!" the little boy demanded. His father carefully leaned forward and the child gingerly delivered a loud, smacking kiss near the wound above his eye.

"Ah," said Greg. "It feels better already. Thank you, William."

The little boy nodded with satisfaction and moved away again.

Reese felt a surprising tightness in his chest. He could barely remember Amalie at that age; Kent and Julie had died mere months before and he had still been trying to adjust to the role of father. Without a lot of success, he added mentally. The little girl had been withdrawn and silent for months after her parents died. It had been more than a year before the two of them had begun to really adjust to their new family status.

He glanced at Celia without quite realizing that he wanted to share the touching moment with her, but she wasn't looking at him. Instead she was watching little William as he toddled off with a toy in his hand. There was such naked pain on her face that he nearly reached for her before he caught himself. Checking Roma, he caught her watching, as well, and when her gaze flashed his, he saw that Celia's friend was fighting tears.

It was then that he realized why Celia had tried to decline Roma's invitation. It hadn't been reluctance to have him get to know her friends. He'd been ridiculously self-centered in coming to that conclusion. She simply hadn't wanted to open the door and admit the pain and loss she lived with every day. He mentally kicked himself around the room. How could he not have realized the impact that a small child—much less a houseful of them—would have on her? And hadn't she told him her son would have started kindergarten this fall? Roma's oldest child looked to be about that age. Talk about rubbing salt in a wound.

He took deep breaths, feeling extraordinarily agitated. He couldn't stand the thought of her suffering like that. Without thinking, he sprang to his feet. "Listen," he commanded.

Everyone in the room except for the smallest child fell silent and turned expectantly to him. Avoiding Celia's gaze, he spoke to Roma. "That wind is getting stronger by the minute. We'd better take a rain check on that dinner invitation, Roma, if you don't mind. I'm afraid we're asking for trouble if we stay much longer."

"You're welcome to weather the storm here with us," Greg offered.

"No," Roma said. "Celia feels just like I do. If something's going to happen to my house, I want to be there to straighten it out right away." She had looked away but then glanced back at Reese as she spoke, and he saw approval in her eyes. She knew exactly what he was doing.

"Reese is right," Celia added. She handed the baby's spoon back to Roma's mother and stood, leaning forward to press a kiss to the little one's forehead. "We'd better go while we still can."

The baby's little face screwed up and she immediately started to fuss.

"Well, at least let me send some chowder along with you," Roma said above the din. She quickly ladled soup into a large jar, screwed the lid on tight and wrapped it in a dishtowel. "That should keep it from burning you," she said as Reese put it in the pocket of the capacious oilcloth raincoat Celia had given him before they'd set out.

"Thanks," Celia told her.

"Thank *you,*" Roma said. "I'd never have gotten everything done in time by myself." She stretched up and planted a light kiss on Reese's cheek as Celia moved off to say her goodbyes to the rest of the family. "Thank you," she said quietly. "I opened my mouth before I thought."

"Yeah, but you did it for the right reasons." They grinned at each other.

"Get her home safely."

"Don't worry." Reese smiled down at Celia's best friend, absurdly pleased at her apparent acceptance of his return to Celia's life. As Celia came to stand beside him again, his gaze caught and held hers for a long moment. "She's not going to get away from me."

A few moments later they stepped out into the storm again.

"Yikes," said Celia. "You were right about the wind getting worse."

Reese took her hand, bending his head against the stinging pellets of rain hurled at them by the blast of the wind. "Did you think I was kidding?"

"No," she said, "but I did think you might be exaggerating as a way to get me out of there faster." She squeezed his hand. "Thank you."

"You're welcome." The wind was making it difficult to converse without shouting. "You can thank me again once we're home."

That startled a laugh from her and they fought their way the short distance back to Celia's sturdy house.

They hung their dripping slickers in her mudroom and hustled into the warmth of her kitchen. Reese set the clam chowder on the butcher-block counter and they worked together to assemble a small meal, which they carried in and set on the low glass-topped driftwood table in front of her large fireplace made of water-smoothed stone.

"We'll have to let the fire burn down soon," she said as they lingered over coffee afterward, "because the wind will start driving the smoke back into the house."

Reese surveyed her, nestled into a mound of pillows with a cranberry-colored woven blanket draped across her lap. "That's all right," he said. "There are other ways to keep warm."

"Reese…"

"Celia…" he teased. He rose, holding her gaze, and he saw her swallow visibly. "Let's clean up these dishes."

Her eyes widened. She chuckled then, tossing a balled-up napkin at him as she rose and began to stack their plates. "You like keeping me off balance," she accused as she brushed past him into the kitchen.

He followed her with a second load. "That's because I live in hope that you'll fall into my arms."

Celia set down the dishes and moved aside so he could do the same. "Reese," she said, her voice troubled, "we just had this discussion. You've been here less than a week. I know I invited you to stay here during the storm, but…we barely know each other."

He made a rough sound of denial and moved forward, capturing her waist in his hands. "That's not true and you know it. We knew each other about as well as any two people on the planet thirteen years ago and I don't think either of us has changed that much." He took her hand and lifted it, pressing her palm flat over his chest. "You still make my heart beat faster," he said. "And I still want you as much as I ever did."

Her face softened and he felt some of the tension leave her body. "You always know exactly what to say, don't you?"

"Only to you." His voice sounded rough and rusty even to his own ears. Slowly he gathered her closer until there was no space between their bodies. "I have missed you so damn much," he said.

"I missed you, too." She brought her hands up to cradle his face as he dropped his head and sought her mouth. Her response to his kiss was everything he'd imagined during the many fantasies he'd had in which they met again. But there was one difference—he'd lost the desire to hurt her as she'd hurt him.

He pressed the tip of a finger to her lips, accepting the instant current of electric attraction that arced between them when he touched her. Then he walked her backward across the room, deliberately letting his body bump hers with each step.

She stopped when she came up against the wall, and her hands flattened on his chest. "What are you doing?"

He ignored the question as he slipped one arm around her and pulled her against him, sliding the other up to cradle her jaw. "I've never been able to forget you."

Her eyes closed. "I know the feeling." Her voice was rueful. Then her palms slid slowly from his chest up to his shoulders, and she leaned into him, laying her head in the curve of his neck.

Euphoria rushed through him as her breath feathered a warm kiss of arousal down his spine. The memory of the kiss they'd shared last night had simmered in the back of his mind all day, of the way she'd softened and let herself relax against him. It was the same thing she'd always done years ago, as if the moment he touched her she became his and his alone. It was an intense turn-on and he wondered if she had any idea how it made him feel when she made that soft sound of acquiescence. Her body aligned with his perfectly when she stood on her toes, and when he'd had her lying open and trusting on his lap, it had been all he could do to restrain himself from yanking open his own pants, stripping hers off and fitting himself into the soft, wet warmth of her spread legs.

Tonight he wasn't going to walk away without finishing this.

Six

Reese threaded one hand into her hair and tugged her head up from his neck, nuzzling along her jaw to her mouth. As his lips slid onto hers, she opened her mouth eagerly, and with that welcome, his tenuous control fell away.

He ran his hands down her back and pulled her hard against him, feeling the full weight of her breasts press into his chest. She'd had beautiful breasts thirteen years ago and he was fairly sure they were even more lovely now. They'd certainly felt fine last night, though it had been too dark for the thorough inspection he longed to make. As she wrapped her arms around his neck and wriggled herself closer, he tugged up the short T-shirt she wore and laid his hand against the smooth, warm flesh of her midriff.

She didn't protest or draw away and he realized that since last night she'd come to some kind of peace, some decision about letting him back into her life. Encouraged and incredibly aroused, he let the shirt ride up over his wrist and forearm and he slid his hand steadily higher until his fingers touched the lacy edge of her bra. The underside of her breast rested on his knuckles and he raised his hand and brushed back and forth over the tip of her breast beneath the fabric.

Celia moaned. She drew back and he knew a crushing disappointment, until she yanked the T-shirt over her head and threw it on the floor. Her eyes met his and her gaze was clear and steady as she stood before him in a black bra that did next to nothing to conceal breasts that were fuller and even more lovely than he remembered. When her hands drifted to the bottom of his own T-shirt, he was galvanized into action and he tore it over his head and let it drop even as his hands reached around her to unclasp her bra.

Her eyelids flickered as the fabric came away. He hooked his fingertips beneath the straps and pulled it down and off so that her breasts fell free and unfettered, swaying gently with each gulp of breath she took. Her nipples were a dusky copper, large and dark, and he groaned, bringing both hands up to fill his palms with the silky globes.

He'd been missing her for so many years and until this moment he hadn't allowed himself to truly think about what it was he'd missed. She was looking down at his hands and she lifted her own, covering his palms and pressing them hard against her flesh. ''Touch me,'' she whispered.

He *was* touching her, but it wasn't enough and he knew exactly what she meant. Releasing her breasts, he put his arms around her and drew her against him, skin to skin, and they both murmured at the intense pleasure in the contact. He bent his head and sought her mouth, and the passionate kiss they exchanged sent fiery streamers of desire streaking through his body, demanding more, more, more.

He lifted her into his arms without breaking the kiss and carried her to the wide sofa in front of the old stone fireplace. On the rug, he stood her on her feet again. He wanted her naked, wanted to touch every gently curving inch, wanted to explore her secrets, to wallow in the familiar and to discern the changes the years had wrought. He unsnapped her pants and tugged them down, slipping his thumbs into the black cotton bikini briefs she wore and taking them off in the same motion. They pooled around her ankles and he took a moment to slip her feet out of her shoes and socks, then sat back on his heels and looked up the length of her.

Her face grew pink. She made an involuntary gesture as if to cover herself and he chuckled, catching her wrists and holding them at her sides. "Don't. I want to see you." He leaned forward and pressed a kiss to the soft curve of her belly, just above the dark tangle of curls. "How can you still be so beautiful?"

She laughed, although the sound was strained. "I have stretch marks." But her hands gently sifted through his hair, scratching lightly over his scalp and sending shivers of arousal through him. "You've got on too many clothes."

He rose. "That can be fixed." He pulled her hands toward him and set them at the buckle of his belt. "Help me."

She looked down, concentrating on the task, and he sucked in a harsh breath at the feel of her fingers against his stomach. Slowly she opened the belt and pulled it wide, then undid the front button of his khaki pants. He was so hard and ready that his clothing was uncomfortable, and when her small fingers gently slid down the tab of his zipper, he had to steel himself against the surge of pressure that threatened his control.

Quickly he reached down and captured her hands, forcing a smile when she looked up at him inquiringly. "Not a good idea right now," he informed her. "I'll take it from here."

She smiled, and he dispensed with the pants and briefs in one smooth motion before straightening and holding out his hand to her. Celia's eyes were wide and shadowed as she looked first at his body, then at the hand he extended. But finally she smiled at him as she linked her fingers through his, and he felt a tension evaporate that he hadn't even fully recognized. As a wave of relief rolled through him, he pulled her against him.

Her body was long and sleek and beautifully muscled from the active work that was a part of her normal routine. She felt so familiar that his throat tightened with an unexpected surge of emotion and he closed his eyes before she could see his reaction. How had he managed to live without her all these years? Not just her body, although as her soft belly cradled his hard, aching flesh between them, he thanked God for it, but the way she smiled at him from beneath her eyelashes, her sly sense of humor, the way she threw herself wholeheartedly into anything she did.

Her hands ran over the solid muscles of his arms and back and she couldn't help but compare his body

with the one she'd known so long ago. There was
nothing left of the boy in him now. Even his shoulders seemed broader. This was a man beneath her
searching fingers—a heavily muscled, hairy-chested,
undeniably aroused man.

He gathered her against him, palming her head in
one large hand and holding her against his shoulder
while he kissed her deeply, repeatedly, teasing her
with his tongue while his free hand slid from her
shoulder to her breast, catching the taut nipple between two fingers. Gently he pinched and rolled until
she could barely stand, her whole body trembling
with the need that shot down to pool between her
legs, and she clutched at his arms. "Please," she said.
"Now."

"What's your rush?" He laughed, a low, growling
sound, as he trailed his lips along the line of her throat
and down the slope of her breast, and she cried out
as his mouth took her in, suckling strongly. Her back
arched and his hand stroked a path down her torso,
spreading wide over her ribs, dipping lightly into the
well of her navel, then brushing with the lightest of
feather touches over the curls between her legs. She
pushed her hips forward, wordlessly begging him, and
suddenly she felt the sharp shock of one long finger
sliding down, testing, tracing, gradually opening her
as he'd done the night before, and she moaned, pressing her face against his shoulder. Her body trembled
in the grip of sensual pleasure; her breath came in
short pants.

Then she felt his finger again, slick and moist,
seeking and pressing against the very heart of her,
and her whole body jerked. She lifted her head from
his shoulder and looked down, exulting in the contrast

of his darkly tanned skin lying against her lighter flesh in that private part, loving the way he cupped her so carefully, aroused by the sight of his hand covering the dark curls there. She moved her hips against his finger and he immediately took up a rhythm, rubbing and circling the locus of her desire as she writhed against him.

Pleasure built swiftly, inexorably carrying her higher and higher. The world shrank as her whole being focused on the big hand controlling her, inciting her response. She sank her teeth into his shoulder, muffling the sounds she made as her hips shifted into a faster, primitive beat that could have only one conclusion.

Suddenly he thrust his hand forward, grinding his palm hard against her as one finger sank deeply into her and she screamed, throwing her head back as her whole body convulsed, reacting to the intense pleasure of the invasion.

"That's it," he muttered against her throat. "That's what I want." He touched her deeply, intimately, until she was a boneless heap of throbbing female moaning softly in his arms.

Finally she opened her eyes. Reese was staring down at her, his eyes brilliant slits of desire. He still cradled her body, his hand still nestled between her thighs. A fine tremor of tension shivered through his body and she drowsily lifted her arms, encircling his neck, lying her head against his shoulder. He bent and lifted her, laying her full length on the rug and coming down beside her.

Somehow the horizontal position seemed even more intimate than what had come before, although she knew that was just plain silly. He lay propped beside her, one leg bent and lying half over hers, and she could feel the very real need that surged through him pulsing at her thigh.

Celia swallowed. Milo had been thin and wiry, slim and slight…all over. The hard shaft pressing against her hip couldn't be called slight in any sense of the word. She'd forgotten, or more likely, if she was truthful, hadn't allowed herself to remember Reese's solid build and how small and feminine she'd always felt in his arms. He shifted, bringing his full weight over her, supporting himself on his forearms, and she felt the first stirrings of panic. She was remembering, too, how uncomfortable their early lovemaking had been until they'd both learned to give her time to adjust to him.

"Reese, wait."

"I've waited long enough." His gaze was fierce and intense, burning with desire as he tore open a condom and quickly rolled it into place, but even then he recognized her unease and sought to allay it. His features softened slightly and he gave her a crooked smile as he pulled her into his arms again. "You're ready, baby. Trust me."

And she did. He moved forward, guiding himself to her, and she sucked in a sharp breath as she felt the blunt, probing force steadily invading her most private place.

"Slowly," she breathed into his ear. "It's been a long time."

He tensed against her, buttocks tight beneath her stroking palms. "And you're just a little thing."

She relaxed, realizing that he understood and remembered the source of her hesitation. "I'm not sure that I'm the one who's unusually sized."

He gave a snort of laughter and she felt him push another small increment deeper. It didn't hurt, and she opened her legs wider, inviting him in as he said, "As I recall, once we got the hang of it, you didn't seem to mind."

"I didn't." She was intoxicated with the sexual innuendo, overwhelmed now with memories, and she playfully reached down between them, curling her hand around him. "I won't." She stroked him lightly and he shuddered.

"Whoa." His voice sounded choked. "I'm trying to make this last, woman."

"Why?" She didn't stop. "We can start all over again as soon as we like."

"There's a thought." With that, he reached down and took her hand away. Holding her gaze, he pushed himself steadily forward, forward, forward, until Celia was gasping and he was lodged deeply within her. He stopped and looked down at her, and her heart turned over at the tenderness in his gaze. "I was afraid I might never get to do this again," he said in a low tone.

Then he twined his fingers with hers, supporting himself on his elbows and holding her hands to the rug.

And he began to move.

How could I have forgotten this?

Celia fought tears, overcome by the wonder of the feelings that flared, new and familiar at the same time, as he established a strong, steady rhythm, advancing and retreating, building another small fire inside her that quickly threatened to explode as his rhythm disintegrated into a frantic maelstrom of movement. He pounded into her, their slick, wet bodies making a satisfying slap with each surge, his breathing hoarse gasps in her ear, his heart thundering against hers.

She could feel herself gathering into a taut knot of need, writhing beneath him as she wrapped her legs around his waist. He touched every part of her with each stroke and as the pace increased, she began to moan again, then to cry out until finally she reached her peak a second time and her body bucked wildly in his arms. Her release triggered his, and with a rough groan of pleasure, Reese finally shuddered and arched against her, his strength shoving her hard against the rug until he slowly relaxed, slumping over her heavily.

After a long moment, he heaved himself onto his elbows again, then dropped his head and sought her lips for a gentle kiss. "No wonder I couldn't forget you," he said. "This was meant to be."

Then he rolled to one side and gathered her into his arms, her back to his front, spoon fashion.

She was lying there, trying to decide how to respond to his statement, when she realized that he was fast asleep.

She lay there for a while, listening to the wind howl around the cottage, feeling safe and secure and happier than she'd been in a long, long time.

This was meant to be.

Was he right? Could it be that easy?

He whistled all the way back down to the marina the next morning. Even the sight of the mess the hurricane had left couldn't dampen his mood. At the last minute the full brunt of the storm had moved off to the east, out to sea, and though the Cape had taken a beating, there didn't appear to be widespread destruction, just a whole lot of annoying junk to clean up.

He'd promised to help Celia with marina repairs—

Celia. He could almost feel his chest swell like a cartoon character guzzling spinach. She made him feel as if he were ten times the man he'd been before he'd found her again.

And he'd better quit mooning around and get busy or he'd never get anything done.

The first thing he did after getting to his boat and finding everything still undamaged was to call Velva and Amalie to let them know that he was all right. The sound of his daughter's cheery little voice lifted his spirits even higher. He missed her like crazy but he wasn't really worried anymore. The kid sounded happy and busy and much too well-adjusted to make herself sick missing him. He couldn't wait to introduce her to Celia.

After the phone call ended, he showered and changed, then went topside for a closer look around the harbor. He was just about to head for the harbormaster's shack to see if Celia had arrived yet when a shocked cry and a rising murmur of distressed voices had him turning in the opposite direction.

Debris littered the coastline. Down the shore a short way, a knot of people in small boats gathered around a stand of grass. He hopped a ride with a guy in a canoe and they headed over to see what was wrong.

As they neared the site, the other man yelled, "What's the matter?"

"There's a body here," said a woman who sounded as though she was one step away from losing it altogether. "I came along here to retrieve some stuff that got away and there she was."

"Guess she got caught in the storm and washed into the water," said another man, shaking his head. "Young, too. Anybody know her?"

Reese gazed down on the battered body wedged into the marsh grass. The woman's long blond hair floated eerily around her head. Her limbs were tangled in a fishing skein that had gotten caught on a dead tree stump and held the body in place when the storm surge receded. The body was facedown, features hidden, clad in a torn bathing suit top and ragged cutoff jeans.

As he studied her, he realized the man who'd just spoken had missed one critical detail. The woman might have gotten caught in the storm all right, but that wasn't what had caused her death. A neat bullet hole in the barely visible right temple probably had been responsible for it.

Just then, a strong wave lapped against the grass and the body did a graceful roll. The hair streamed back in the undertow, exposing a ghostly pale face. Reese swore.

The body in the fishing net was Claudette Mason.

Celia felt numb with disbelief. Claudette was dead. And she hadn't died in a storm-related accident. She'd been murdered in cold blood. Whoever had done it clearly hadn't expected her body to be found. The fishing skein had been wrapped around her too neatly to have been accidental, and it was torn in places that suggested that it had been weighted. Investigators theorized that the force of the hurricane had torn the body from the weights and left it tangled in the marsh.

Celia sat quietly in a corner of her office as two FBI agents questioned members of her staff. Angie was answering a query at the moment, telling the two men that she had seen Claudette walking around Neil Brevery's yacht the morning before the storm, but that they hadn't spoken.

"I can't believe it," Angie said, a lone tear streaking down her cheek. "Murders just don't *happen* here." Then, as if realizing what she'd said, her eyes darted to Celia in silent apology.

"We believe Miss Mason may have been involved in a drug transaction," said the taller, older agent. "As you know, Harwichport was the focal point for drug activity several years ago and the DEA has acquired recent evidence that suggests it hasn't ceased."

"What evidence?" Did they know things they hadn't told her? Celia understood, on an intellectual basis, that the FBI couldn't go around blabbing their information to civilians, but her interest was far from casual and they knew how she felt. She hadn't had any idea they were still actively investigating in the area.

"Sorry, Mrs. Papaleo, we can't discuss an ongoing investigation." The younger agent sounded sincere. He and his partner had spoken with her a number of times after Milo's boat exploded, so she was familiar with them. "We'll let you know personally if there's any new information released."

That evening Reese walked her home and they made dinner together while they discussed the bizarre turn the day had taken. Celia seemed jittery and upset and he imagined that Claudette Mason's shocking death had stirred up a great many memories she'd prefer to have left at rest. He could only be thankful she hadn't been with him when the body was discovered.

They sat down afterward to watch the news and he wondered if she would let him stay tonight. He put his arm around her and she turned to him, smiling and snuggling into his side in a motion so natural it felt as if she'd done it for years.

Stretching up, she put her mouth against his jaw, and he could feel her hot breath feather over his neck as she said, "Would you like to stay tonight?"

He grinned, tilting his head and catching her mouth beneath his. "Would you believe I was just plotting a way to do exactly that?"

Her lips curved as she shifted in his arms, her hands sliding up over his shoulders. "I'd believe it."

Much later, they lay together in her bed. Moonlight silvered a patch across the quilt over them.

In the darkness he felt melancholy steal over him. They could have been married for years by now, with children of their own. If he hadn't left. If she had gotten in touch. "We've lost so much time," he said quietly.

She hesitated, her palm creeping up to lie over his heart. "Yes."

"When did you first hear the rumors?"

As he'd expected, she knew what he meant. "About a week after you left. People started saying...that you'd gotten a girl pregnant." Her voice shook.

"Yeah." He still couldn't prevent the hurt that had sliced at him that day from echoing in his voice. "The worst thing was, my father didn't even consider that maybe I hadn't done it. He *assumed* I was the father of that baby. Do you know he actually thought he could force me to marry her?'' He shook his head. ''We had the mother and father of all fights. I swore I was never setting foot in that house again until he apologized. But now…now I realize I was as unfair as he was. I didn't just shun Dad. I left my entire family.''

He sighed. ''Being back here with you, realizing this is the life I should have had, makes me miss them so damn much. It doesn't seem nearly as important to me anymore to hang on to all that anger. What do you think? Should I extend the olive branch and forget about the apology?''

Celia's body stiffened again, surprising him. He hadn't thought the question was that big a deal. He tried to hold her but she struggled until he let her go.

Pushing herself out of his arms, she sat up and turned slightly to face him. ''Reese, I owe you an apology.'' She took a deep breath. ''When I heard about the other woman's pregnancy, I was shattered. And when you left without even getting in touch, I was so hurt. I…''

Her voice began to recede as incredulity crept in. *She hadn't believed in him.* All these years, that had been the one equation he'd never figured. Never considered.

''You believed it. You believed it, didn't you?'' The ugly truth was beginning to register and his voice was harsh. He surged out of bed, yanked on his shorts and plunged one hand recklessly through his hair, leaving short spikes sticking out at wild, stiff angles. ''All these years you thought I was the kind of guy who would tell you he loved you at the same time he was screwing around with somebody else.''

"Well, what was I supposed to think?" she shouted.

She clapped a hand to her mouth, clearly appalled at her loss of control. Then her defiant gaze dropped and she pulled the sheet up, concealing her body from him as if she were no longer comfortable with the intimacy they'd shared.

"Reese, I was a very naive seventeen-year-old. You tell me you're going back to Boston to start school but that you'll be coming back the following weekend. The next thing I know, everyone's buzzing about you getting some girl pregnant and having a big fight with your father—and I never hear another word!"

"The letters weren't good enough, I guess," he said sarcastically. "You didn't waste any time writing me off."

"Letters?" Her head came up and her face was a study in troubled disbelief. She shook her head. "I never received any letters from you."

He went still. Hurt continued to slice through him, and he fought the urge to hurl words at her in return. But there had been a note of truth in her tone that he couldn't ignore. "Celia, I sent you three letters. If you never received them, then…someone kept them from you."

She stared at him, silent and clearly shocked, and he could see in her eyes the dawning of a terrible truth. "Oh my God," she whispered. She shook her head blindly. "My father wouldn't have— Daddy would never— Oh, God!" She buried her face in her hands. "He worried about me that summer," she said in a muffled tone. "He was a good man, despite the drinking. But if he thought…he might have…" She raised her face and Reese saw in her expression a sad resignation. "My father kept them from me. What did the letters say?"

He shrugged, still cut to the quick at the way she'd condemned him without a second thought, just like his own family. What was the use in getting into this now? "Nothing important."

Celia went still, studying his face. "Please, Reese," she said quietly. "What was in those letters?"

"An explanation." He turned away abruptly, walking to the window and placing his hands on the windowsill, leaning forward until his head nearly touched the glass. "My first impulse was to run to you. But even before I picked up the phone, I realized my father would like nothing better. If he'd been able to catch me in a compromising position with an underage girl, he could have used the threat of statutory rape charges to force me to do what he wanted."

Celia's eyes went wide. "Surely your father wouldn't have done that."

His mouth twisted. "Looking back, probably not. But I wasn't exactly thinking clearly. So I took off, left the States. That's when I wrote the first letter, telling you I'd be back the day of your eighteenth birthday."

She made a stifled sound, bringing her fisted hand to her lips.

"In the second letter, I told you about starting my trip around the world. I hadn't heard from you yet, so I wrote again and asked you if you'd marry me. But I never got an answer."

Celia fought to hold back the tears. Dear God. She'd thought she was nothing more than summer entertainment to him. How could she have been so wrong? "Oh, Reese, if only I'd known. I'm so sorry."

"Forget about it." He still faced the window but she didn't need to see his face to know she'd unknowingly hurt him. "It was for the best. I got to see the world. I made buckets of money and I did whatever I damn well pleased for more than a dozen years. If I'd tied myself to you, I might still be stuck here."

She flinched as the cold words slapped her. But behind them, she heard the pain. He'd been rejected by his family, and then he'd thought she'd done the same thing. When he'd realized how easily she'd accepted his guilt, it must have compounded the betrayal he must have felt. She'd give anything if she could turn the clock back and fix it.

Getting out of bed, she went to him, slipping her arms around his waist and pressing herself against him, heedless of her nudity. "I'm sorry," she said, pressing a kiss to the center of his strong back and speaking against the warm flesh. "I should have believed in you. I have no excuse for it, and I'll regret it until the day I die."

He stiffened noticeably beneath her touch and she clutched at him more tightly, prepared for rejection. But she wasn't prepared when he said, "Look! Look out there and tell me what you see."

He grasped her wrist and pulled her around in front of him, placing his hands on her shoulders as she looked out the window across the darkened water, visible from her second story. Her eyes were already acclimated to the dark and it was only a moment before she saw what he had. "It's some kind of small yacht, running without lights, I think." She whirled and ran from the room, rummaging in the closet for her binoculars, which she quickly opened and handed to Reese.

"It is," he said. "Definitely. And it looks very much like it just came out of your harbor."

She sucked in a breath of outrage. "I'm calling the FBI first thing in the morning."

Reese put a cautionary hand on her arm. "Celia, we need to make sure no one finds out we saw this. Claudette's murder most likely proves they're still here. These people apparently don't consider either of us a danger or we'd be dead by now, too." His thumbs caressed her forearms lightly. "I know it goes against the grain, but you need to be careful about stirring this particular hornet's nest. They've already proven they can be lethal."

"We can't let them keep using my harbor," she said hotly.

"Celia," he said patiently, "I'm not telling you to ignore it. I'm just saying we need to be careful." He set down the binoculars and put his hands at her waist, drawing her to him. "I won't take chances with your life."

"What happened to 'it was for the best'?" She kept her tone light, trying to let him know she understood the hurt that drove him to lash out.

Reese grimaced. "I was mad, okay? Even after all these years, it still hurt to think that you didn't trust me. But knowing you never got my letters…I guess if I'd been in your shoes I might have thought the same thing." His fingers tightened on her waist. "I don't know if we can sort out everything that's behind us, and I don't know if I care." He snuggled her closer. "What I do care about is us, right now. And I'm not going to throw that away. We've already missed too many days we should have shared."

When he bent his head again, she met his mouth with urgent desire, needing to show him that she cared, too. Unlike Reese, who seemed to have it all figured out, she wasn't sure where this was going or how it would end. But Reese had made her *feel* for the first time since Leo and Milo had died, and she wasn't giving that up without a fight.

Seven

"It's so horrible," Angie said as they restored the office equipment to its proper place the next afternoon.

Celia nodded. "I know. Poor Claudette."

"And it's scary, too. There could be a murderer right here on this pier."

"There could be."

"Do you think there is?"

"I don't really have any idea." She put an arm around Angie's shoulders briefly. "But I want you to try not to worry so much about it. The FBI is doing everything possible to catch these people."

"That's what we all said the last time," Angie said baldly.

Celia flinched and Angie's expression immediately switched to regret.

"I'm sorry," she said. "This just has me so on edge."

"We're all on edge. The only thing to do is keep on with our normal routine and let the professionals do their job. And speaking of which—" she flipped the schedule on the desk around so that she could read it "—did you have any small craft out last night?"

Angie hesitated, apparently thinking. "No. Everything was returned by six. Why?"

Celia shrugged. "I just wondered." She made a show of checking the list. "So today we have two all-day charters and three small group rentals?"

"Yes." Angie leaned in to check, but then she straightened. "I almost forgot. A guy just docked a few minutes ago. He asked for Reese, but there was nobody aboard the *Amalie.* I came in to see if you knew where he was."

"He walked down to the video store," Celia said. "Who's the guy?"

"Don't know, but if I had to guess, I'd bet he was a Barone. He looks a little like Reese, and his boat is the *Baronessa.*"

Reese's brother. Celia leaped to her feet and headed for the door. She'd forgotten that Nicholas Barone had been on the Cape. The Barones rarely used her little marina, preferring Saquatucket, which was closer to the family compound. She was willing to bet Nick Barone turning up at Harwichport wasn't a coincidence.

As she hurried down the pier, Ernesto Tiello was walking toward her. He moved slowly, like a very old man, and she suddenly remembered the way he'd followed Claudette Mason around like an eager puppy. Her heart squeezed with pity.

"Mr. Tiello," she said as he drew nearer. "I'm so sorry about what's happened to Claudette. I know you two were close."

Tiello's face was drawn and haggard, and deep in his eyes she saw a flare of pain at her words. "Yes," he said, dropping his gaze to the ground. "We had become good friends. Her death has been...most difficult."

Impulsively she reached out a hand and squeezed his shoulder. "Is there anything I can do?"

He shook his head without looking at her. "There is nothing to be done. Except, perhaps, allow the authorities to do their job and catch whoever did this."

She nodded, agreeing. "I hope they're successful." Looking past Ernesto's portly frame, she noticed that a tall man with dark hair and shoulders as broad as Reese's was coming her way. "Please excuse me," she said to the distraught man. "If there's any way I can help you, please don't hesitate to ask."

"Thank you." Ernesto Tiello moved on past her and she walked along the dock toward the stranger who was rapidly approaching.

She extended a hand as she came to a halt in front of him. "I'm Celia Papaleo, the harbormaster. I understand you're looking for Reese."

"Celia." His eyes were full of knowledge as he clasped her hand in a firm grip. "Nick Barone." He paused and studied her for a moment. "The same Celia who used to date my brother?"

She nodded. "The same."

"And how about now?"

"Excuse me?"

"Are you dating him now?"

She hesitated, wondering how to answer him. Dating? Not exactly. But...

"Never mind. That was rude." He grinned and her heart skipped a beat; that smile was a close relative to the one Reese employed when he was teasing her. "Do you happen to know where he is?"

"He walked down to the video store. Would you like to come into my office to wait for him?" She turned and gestured toward the shack and they walked up the pier, but before she could show him inside, a familiar figure came striding toward them.

"Reese!" she called, wanting to give him time to...

To what? Compose himself? Brace himself? Get himself under control? "Your brother stopped by."

Just for a moment, she detected a slight hesitation in his smooth gait. But he recovered quickly and came toward them, his face blank and unreadable. He extended his hand. "Nick. It's been a long time."

There was a frozen moment and then Nick Barone grabbed his brother's hand and hauled him into a hard embrace. "You damned idiot," he said. "Your quarrel's with Dad, not with me." He pounded Reese's back. "God, I've missed you."

Celia turned away to hide the tears she couldn't suppress. She knew how much Reese missed his family; this unconditional love was exactly what he'd needed.

Behind her, Reese said, "I've missed you, too." His voice sounded thick.

"So why in hell didn't you answer my letters?"

She turned back, alarmed at the frustration and strain in Nick Barone's voice. If he thought she was going to stand by and let him hurt Reese even further, he could think again.

Reese shrugged, stepping back a pace. "I don't know."

She could sense him backing off mentally, as well, and before either of the brothers could do something stupid, she said, "Nick, would you like to join us for dinner tonight? That will give you plenty of time to catch up."

Two sets of eyes turned her way. One was a piercing blue while the other was a steely silver, but two nearly identical gazes pinned her like a butterfly to a mat. She could almost see each of them thinking.

Finally, Nick said, "Thank you. I'd like that…if my brother doesn't mind."

Reese cleared his throat. "Of course I don't mind. Let's make it seven o'clock since Celia will be here most of the afternoon."

Reese heard her feet on the porch an instant before the back door opened.

"Hi," she said when she saw him standing in her kitchen. Then she sniffed. "What is that? Smells great."

"Stuffed baked chicken breasts in wine sauce. And a spinach salad." He handed her a glass of the Fume Blanc he'd picked up on his way over to start dinner. "But I forgot dessert. Shall I run back out to the store?"

"No." She set down her bag and left her shoes by the door. "I have a pumpkin loaf in the freezer that can be cut and served after a five-minute defrost. That'll do, won't it?"

Reese set down the cutlery with which he'd been

about to set the table. He walked toward her and took her hands, tugging her against him for a sweet kiss. She opened her mouth beneath his so willingly that he felt an immediate rise of desire, and more. God, he loved the way she responded to him. He'd dreamed of this for thirteen years, and now that she was finally his again, he could hardly believe it.

Slipping his arms around her, he said, "Pumpkin loaf sounds great. And now we have all kinds of extra time since we don't have to worry about dessert." He lowered his head and kissed her again, hungrily drinking in her response, stroking her soft, lithe curves possessively. "Wonder what we could do to fill the hours."

Laughter gurgled up out of her throat. "Gee, I don't know." She slid one hand down his body, her small palm covering the hard evidence of arousal that pushed at the front of his pants, and smiled when he shuddered. "We'll think of something."

As he carried her up the stairs, she wound her fingers into his hair and cradled his scalp. "I was afraid you might be mad at me."

"For what?"

"For inviting your brother to dinner."

"Oh." He shrugged. "At first I was a little annoyed, but then I realized I really wanted to have dinner with him, so I couldn't be mad, could I?" He dropped his head and kissed her. "Thank you."

She responded to him with all the sweetness he remembered from their loving years ago, her body rising to meet his. As he stroked and petted her, she writhed beneath him with complete abandon, stoking

the fires of passion until she flared into a wild con-
flagration that seared his senses and consumed him,
as well.

An hour later they were lying side by side on her
bed. Reese had his arm around her, her bare body
aligned with his, and he lazily stroked her back with
his free hand. She snuggled closer, loving the cuddling, the closeness. Loving him.

She felt the final, small knot of denial loosen and
drift away from the close guards she'd put on her
heart. She loved Reese Barone. Had she ever stopped
loving him?

No. She'd buried it, said goodbye to her girlish
dreams of a life with Reese after he'd left. But the
feeling had never died. Now he was back and there
was no way to deny it. She loved him, had always
loved him. *Would* always love him, until the day she
stopped breathing.

A rush of emotion swept through her and she
turned her head so that she could press a kiss to the
hard pad of muscle over his heart. *I love you.*

Reese's arm tightened around her. "I don't remember you being so noisy years ago." His words interrupted her moment of introspection. He grinned as
she balled a fist and delivered a punch to his shoulder.
"Not that I'm complaining."

"I was young and inhibited."

"Not too inhibited to make love on a catamaran in
the middle of the day." His free hand tipped up her
chin and he gave her a deep, stirring kiss. "It's one
of my favorite memories."

"Mine, too."

"So you didn't totally forget me." His tone wasn't

smug and satisfied, as she'd expected, but rather diffident.

"Did you really think I could ever forget you?" She shook her head slightly. "You were my whole world that summer."

"And you were mine." He paused. "I, uh, have to tell you something."

She twisted a curl of the hair on his chest around her finger and glanced up at him, alerted by an odd note in his voice. "Oh?"

"I was here briefly at the end of August. I found out you were still around and that's why I came back."

She propped herself up on his chest, her heart aching strangely as his words arranged themselves into meaning in her head. "You came back...to find me?"

He grinned at her, but it wavered around the edges. "Yeah."

"Did you know I was...single?"

He nodded. "Somebody over at Saquatucket mentioned you'd been widowed." He ran his hands lightly up her back. "I just had to know if you really were as special as I remembered."

"It's hard to live up to an idealized thirteen-year-old memory," she said, striving for a light tone.

"Celia." He twisted, lying her flat on the pillow and leaning over her on one elbow, his eyes intense and serious. "You haven't lived up to it."

Shock left her speechless. She supposed she should feel pain, but she didn't—yet.

Then he said, "You've exceeded it. To be honest, I came back hoping, I think, to get you out of my system so I could get on with the rest of my life. Instead—" he paused, stroking a finger along her cheek "—I'm having a hard time imagining what it would be like without you now."

Her throat closed up as her eyes began to sting. Why was it that she couldn't simply enjoy his sweet words? While part of her reveled in knowing that he wanted her as badly as she wanted him, a wary corner of her heart backpedaled. She hadn't planned on caring for anyone ever again, hadn't planned on letting anyone get so close that she'd be devastated if they were torn from her. She might love him, but she realized suddenly that she hadn't allowed herself to consider thoughts of a future with him. The whole notion was so frightening that she simply couldn't face it.

Did she love him? Yes, yes, *yes!* But loving someone was no guarantee of anything, except heartbreak. Conflicting feelings raged within her. *Hide,* said one voice. *Protect your heart.*

Another urged her to tell Reese how she felt. True, he hadn't said the words, but neither had she. And hadn't he just practically admitted that he still cared? His words skirted the edge of a marriage proposal, didn't they?

And with that thought, panic rose. No. No, no, no, she couldn't do it again. Dear God, what would happen if she lost Reese? She'd thought her life was over when Milo and Leo, her precious baby boy, had died. But if Reese died... The mere thought chilled every cell in her body. She couldn't do this. *She couldn't.*

She turned her head to one side, hating the weak tears that seeped from beneath her eyelids. "Reese, I—I don't know. It's not that—"

She felt him freeze against her. "Baby, the last thing I want to do is make you unhappy." He stroked her hair. "One day at a time, remember? If that's what you want, that's what we'll do."

Clearly, it wasn't necessarily what he wanted or needed, but he'd give her space. Thinking of the future was one giant step beyond where she could tread right now.

But how long would Reese tolerate her reticence? How patient could he be? A chill traced icy fingers up her spine. He'd left once before, when she'd never even imagined he would. Now she knew better.

What if he left again?

Nick arrived promptly at seven with a bottle of wine for his hostess, which they opened equally promptly. Celia had prepared a tray with crackers, apples and cheese, and Nick joined Reese in the living room while she returned to the kitchen. Reese watched her leave the room, knowing she was being thoughtful, giving him time for a private reunion, but wishing she were by his side anyway.

Pouring the wine into deep-bowled crystal glasses that Celia had retrieved from a cupboard and hastily washed, Reese handed Nick a glass of Merlot. Nick held the glass by the stem, swirling it competently and eyeing the color before inhaling its bouquet. The last time they'd seen each other, they'd barely been legal, and as Reese recalled, their drink of choice was dark Mexican beer. The contrast served to remind him again of the distance he'd maintained through the years. Once again regret nipped at him.

God, it was good to see Nick. They were only a year apart in age and had been inseparable companions during their childhood, along with the next brother down the line, Joe, who was only a year younger than Reese.

"So, how are you?" He tried not to stare, drinking in the familiar yet different features, measuring the subtle changes adulthood had brought to Nick.

"Good, good. Married."

"Married," Reese repeated. "Celia said she thought you were. Any kids?"

"One. A daughter."

Reese shook his head, again unable to process the changes in his brother. "Not possible."

Nick grinned wickedly, and for an instant their old closeness returned. "Quite possible. Want me to explain it to you?"

Reese returned the smile. "No, thanks. I think I've got it." He hesitated, feeling awkward again. "How'd you find me?"

"Daniel."

Daniel. Reese's cousin, Derrick's twin brother, though the two were as different as two men could be. Reese was genuinely puzzled. "How did Daniel know I was here?" As in here at Celia's.

Nick must have read his mind. "He didn't. He was at the Cape house in August on his honeymoon and when he came home, he told me he was pretty sure he'd caught a glimpse of you." Nick's face tightened. "I thought about it and thought about it and finally decided to come see if he was right."

Reese was astounded by the coincidence. "I was only here for two days that time. Then I went home again—Florida is home, by the way—and arranged for a longer vacation."

"To see Celia."

"To look up Celia," he corrected Nick. "I heard she might be single."

"And obviously, she is. Waited for you all these years, huh?"

Reese realized Nick must not know that Celia was a widow, but he decided not to get into all that for the moment.

"Not exactly," Reese said dryly. He looked straight at Nick. "I was planning to get in touch while I was here. You beat me to it."

"Right." There was the faintest note of derision in his brother's tone.

"I saw Derrick last week, over on Nantucket, and it made me realize how much I wanted to see the rest of you." There was no point in telling Nick everything he'd seen.

"He didn't mention that." Nick looked disgusted. "He's even more of a royal screwup than he was when you were home. I swear he enjoys stirring up trouble."

"I didn't talk to him." Reese spread his hands when Nick's eyebrows rose. "It wasn't a good time and I didn't have a lot to say."

"He'd have probably bent your ear about how badly he's being treated right now," said Nick.

"Meaning?"

"How much have you kept up with what's happening at Baronessa?" Nick stood and began roaming the room, examining Celia's knickknacks and pictures, but Reese got the impression he wasn't really seeing them.

"Not much." Reese stood, too, watching his older brother prowl. "Celia told me someone started a fire. Why would anyone want to burn down the plant?"

"I wish I knew." Nick looked frustrated. "That wasn't the first incident but it's by far the most serious. Someone has a grudge, and I think it's personal."

"The Conti family?" Funny how the word "grudge" immediately brought their grandfather's old rival to mind.

"We don't have any proof of that. But last week the Contis hired a private investigator," Nick said.

"What for?"

His brother shook his head. "Don't know. And believe me, we'd like to. Claudia's been unofficially appointed to try to find out why. And that's got Derrick's boxers in a knot. He thinks he should be in on the investigation of the investigator."

Reese had to smile.

"But you know how abrasive he can be. That hasn't changed in thirteen years. He's the last person I want messing around the Contis, and I finally had to tell him straight out to stay clear of it."

"Bet that went over big."

"Yeah, like mud in a milkshake."

"Celia heard that Emily was hurt in the fire. Is she all right?"

Nick hesitated. "Yes and no. Physically, she's recovered. She wasn't burned, but she had a head injury from falling debris."

Reese winced. "How bad?"

"She's recovered, as I said, but she's experienced some significant memory loss. It's possible that she saw whoever set that fire but she can't remember. Hell, it's possible whoever set that fire intended her to die in there."

"God." He was shaken by the thought.

"The only good thing to come out of it is that the

firefighter who carried Em out of there is her fiancé now."

Her fiancé? He chuckled despite himself, shaking his head. Although he knew it was foolish, it was hard to rid himself of the thirteen-year-old images of his family. "When I left home, she was eleven. How can she possibly be engaged?"

But Nick didn't return the laughter. "We're all grown now. You've been away a long time, Reese."

He sobered quickly in the face of his brother's unspoken censure. "I know how long it's been."

"Why didn't you stay in touch? Answer my letters?"

"I don't know." He looked at the ground. "I was just so pissed…and hurt, more than anything." Funny how he could finally admit that. "I wasn't mad at any of you guys except the old man, but I couldn't…I couldn't see any of you. I had to get away, fast. And once I was gone, time sort of got away from me."

There was hurt, deep hurt, in Nick's gaze, and such reproach that he had to look away again. "It sure did."

There was a heavy silence. He knew it was his fault they'd been out of touch for so long. Early on, several of his siblings had tried to communicate—but he'd been such a jerk. And now they'd lost more than a decade of precious memories that they could never replace. It was only since Kent had died that he could fully appreciate how important shared memories could be. "So tell me about the rest of the gang."

"Mom and Dad are well. They miss you, too," Nick said. He ignored the slight stiffening Reese couldn't prevent and smoothly moved on. "Let's see. I'll just go down the line so I don't forget anyone.

Joe was married and widowed young. It was a terrible thing, but he's married again to a great woman. Colleen became a nun—"

"A nun?" On second thought, he wasn't completely surprised.

"But she left her order a couple years ago and recently got married. Guess who she married?"

Reese raised an eyebrow.

"Gavin O'Sullivan!"

"O'Sullivan! You're kidding." Nick's best friend from childhood had been one of Reese's best buds, as well.

"Nope." Nick ticked off their siblings on his fingers. "Alex is married and a father, Gina's married. Rita's a nurse now and she's married to a doctor."

"And Maria?" He couldn't imagine his youngest sisters all grown up and married.

Nick hesitated. "Maria's…missing."

Missing? "What the hell does that mean?"

"She went away last month. She left a note so we wouldn't worry, but nobody knows where she is."

"Do you think she's okay?"

Nick spread his hands. "I hope so. If she isn't back by the date she promised, I'm calling out the National Guard."

"So how about the cousins?"

"Cousins!" The worry fell away from Nick's face and he actually laughed. "Derrick, Daniel and Em I already mentioned. And Claudia…Claudia is a force of nature. Still single, totally gorgeous and as bullheaded as ever. But here's a shocker. We have a new cousin!"

Reese was confused. "One of them has a child?"

"Not yet. The new cousin is Uncle Luke's daughter."

He was positively staggered by the news. Their father's twin brother had been abducted from the hospital when they were just two days old, and despite massive efforts by the police, no trace of Luke had ever surfaced. Reese's memories of his grandmother were of a sweet, gentle Italian matriarch with an aura of sorrow that never completely left her eyes. "You guys found Uncle Luke?"

"Not exactly." Nick's face fell. "Turns out he's already passed away. But his daughter, Karen, figured out who she was when some pictures of a family reunion in July made the papers. She got in touch, and now we've got another family member. Several, actually, since she's married with a baby on the way."

"Whoa. Can't wait to meet her."

"Does that mean you're considering coming home?"

Damn. Nick always had been a persistent cuss. "I've thought about visiting," he said cautiously.

"So will you come for a visit? Bring Celia, too, if you guys are serious." When Reese didn't immediately acquiesce, Nick said, "You could stay with us if you don't want to stay at the house."

"I'll think about it." But first he needed to find out what—if any—direction this dance he and Celia were doing was going. *Were* they serious, as Nick put it? He hoped so. Because he'd like nothing better than to have her with him, to introduce her to his family. Preferably as his wife. "I'll think about it," he said again, "and get in touch."

"Reese," Nick said softly, "Dad's sorry about that fight. He's been sorry since the day you left. Mom hardly spoke to him for at least a year. She wanted to hire people to find you but he wouldn't let her. He said if you didn't want to ever see him again he couldn't blame you and that if you wanted to come home, you would.''

Reese stared at his older brother. A bitter wash of regret tasted sour in his throat. ''If he'd ever uttered one word of apology, I'd have been home like a shot,'' he said stiffly. ''But I wasn't coming back so I could be falsely accused and screamed at again.''

''You wouldn't have been,'' Nick informed him. ''Eliza Mayhew confessed that she'd lied about the baby's father. He was some guy from her university. I don't think Dad will ever forgive himself for not trusting you.'' He swallowed. ''Deep down, I believe he thinks he shouldn't ever be forgiven. Living without you is his punishment.'' His mouth twisted. ''Only thing is, it's punished all the rest of us, as well.'' He gave Reese an affectionate punch in the shoulder. ''Jerk.''

''Hey, you two.'' Celia's slim frame was silhouetted in the light streaming into the room from the kitchen. ''The meal's about ready.''

The evening had been surprisingly enjoyable, Reese thought, cuddling her closer in her bed that night. He'd expected more tension. Suppressed anger. There'd been the occasional awkward moment, but all in all, it had been damned good to see his brother again.

Nick had mellowed, somehow. He'd always been intense and driven, but tonight he'd been different. Maybe marriage was responsible. Reese was looking forward to meeting his new wife.

Celia stirred in his arms. "How are you?" Her voice was soft, tentative.

"Good." He kissed her temple. "Seeing Nick was terrific."

"I'm glad. I worried all day that I'd pushed you into something you weren't ready for."

"I didn't think I was," he said reflectively. "Maybe I needed a little nudge in the right direction."

They were silent again. His hand swept up and down her back, stroking the silky skin in a gently abstracted manner as he thought about what he'd just said. Maybe he wasn't the only one who needed a little nudge, he thought.

He cleared his throat. "I haven't really told you, but I'd like to hear about Leo if you ever want to talk about him. I'd like to know about your pregnancy, his birth, what kind of stuff he liked. Anything you'd like to share."

Celia's body went rigid in his arms. "You said his name." Her voice sounded wounded. "Do you know how long it's been since I've heard anyone say his name? Everyone thinks they're helping if they don't remind me, I guess." A sob broke loose and he felt the warmth of tears dampen his skin beneath her cheek. "But it's like he and Milo never existed sometimes."

He pulled her closer, each tear that touched him feeling like a live ember. "They still exist, baby. They'll always live in your memories." He took a deep breath. "Any time you want to talk about them, I'll listen."

She went still in his arms. "That," she finally said, "is an extraordinarily kind offer."

He smiled and kissed the top of her head. "Yeah, considering I'm eaten alive with jealousy when I let myself think that it should have been me you shared those years with, that I should have been your son's father."

Celia's body had gone stiff in his arms again. Well, tough. He was tired of her resisting him. "This is how it should have been all those years ago. We should have gotten married, made a home of our own and started a family." He took her arms and shook her lightly. "I still want those things," he said, tipping up her chin with a relentless hand until she met his eyes.

But she dropped her gaze, closing herself away from him, shielding her thoughts. Quietly she said, "But will you still want me if children aren't a part of the equation?"

Now it was his turn to pause. He should tell her now that he already had a child. But…she'd made it pretty damn clear that she didn't want more children, and he found he couldn't force himself to speak. He needed more time. Time to let her get used to the idea of *them* again, time to cement the bonds of love with the meeting of flesh as well as emotions. She'd loved him once, and he was beginning to be pretty sure she still did.

"I want you any way I can get you," he said in a rough voice. He rolled over, pushing her back against the pillows as he settled himself snugly against her. She made a small, soft noise of approval in her throat and he knew exactly how she felt. They had been made for each other. Making love to her was like finding his own personal miracle.

He stroked the tears from her face with his thumbs.

"Any way at all," he affirmed as he sought her mouth and his hands began to slide over her silky skin.

Sensitive now to her desire not to create scandal, he left in the soft almost-morning light that pearled the sky above the ocean to the east. They kissed on the stoop and he felt like a teenager again.

"Will I see you later?" He still held her loosely against him.

She nodded. "You can join us at the marina if you like. We still have a lot of storm cleanup to take care of."

"Work? Me?" He grinned, and she smiled as he'd intended her to. He drew her to him for one final, lingering kiss. "All right. I suppose I could manage that if I had some incentive."

"Ah," she said against his lips, "have I got an incentive program for you. Why don't you plan on coming over for dinner and we'll discuss it?"

"I have a better idea," he said, running his palms up and down the long, smooth line of her back. "Let's have dinner aboard the yacht tonight. We could sail up the coast and back afterward and enjoy an evening on the water."

She laid her head against his shoulder and he enjoyed the feel of her snuggled against him. "That sounds lovely. Let's do it."

Eight

He visited a local bakery where he'd discovered an incredibly good corn bread made by the proprietor, then bought lobster and shrimp from a fresh fish shack on the waterfront. A salad and one of Celia's apple cobblers would be all they would need.

Except each other, he thought, his blood heating as he thought of the night to come. Then he shook his head, laughing at himself. He was as bad as he'd been during the summer he'd spent with Celia, unable to get enough of her. No matter how many times he made love to her, it seemed all he did was think about the next time he could get her into his bed.

It wasn't just the physical fulfillment, although he had no complaints in that department. No, it wasn't just their lovemaking, but the closeness he craved, both physical and emotional. He'd been without her for so long that he doubted he would ever get enough of simply holding her next to him, feeling her heart's steady beat as her blood coursed through the fragile blue veins at her wrists, her temples and just under the petal-soft skin of her breasts. It delighted him when they finished each other's sentences, when they laughed at the same thing at the same moment, when a mere glance from her could calm and reassure him.

How amazing was it that after thirteen years he'd come back at the right time and found her? If he were inclined to believe in fate, he might think their getting together again had been inevitable. Only this time, the ending was going to be different. He was going to make sure of it.

Suddenly the little detail that he'd kept from her— his daughter—reared up and smacked him full in the face. Panic clutched at his chest.

He had to tell her tonight. He had to. He never should have kept it from her for so long, never should have let things get so serious between them until she knew. Now there could be no easy way to introduce the topic. He could hear himself now.

Oh, by the way, did I mention I have a daughter?

…This boat? Oh, I thought I told you. It's named after my daughter, Amalie.

…Celia, I don't know how to tell you this, but I have a daughter. What? The reason I didn't tell you before? Well, I was sure you'd drop me like a hot potato.

And she just might. There was no excuse for not telling her that he had a child to raise—except that he was a complete and total coward. And he'd been terrified he might lose her. It had seemed smart to get their new relationship off to a solid start before springing the notion of a child on her.

It had seemed smart because he'd been too chicken to let himself think about what might happen and he'd been doing his damnedest to portray an ostrich, hoping that if he stuck his head in the sand, the problem would go away.

Well, no more delays. No more procrastinating.

He had to tell her *tonight*. Because he'd made up his mind to ask her to marry him. He knew how she felt about having children; she'd made no secret of it. And he'd seen her pain with his own eyes. Was it fair to ask her to consider another child?

No. He'd cut off his arm before he'd put her in a position to have her life shattered as it had been once. But it wasn't as if he was asking her to have another baby. A small, sharp pain pinched his heart but he forced himself to ignore it. In an ideal world he would love nothing more than to make Celia his wife and to spend the next few years making babies of their own.

But he'd seen what losing her son had done to her. And he'd rather have Celia with no children than live without her ever again. Raising Amalie was different, he told himself stoutly. Ammie wasn't her biological child.

Oh, he knew that taking on a ready-made family wouldn't be easy for Celia. But once she got used to the idea, they would be happy. She could move to Florida, or he and Am could move up here if she didn't want to leave the Cape.

He took a deep breath. His hands were clammy as he set the small galley table and put a bottle of Riesling on ice. There was a knot, an unpleasant burning sensation lodged dead center in his chest, and he wondered briefly if he'd given himself an ulcer worrying about her reaction to his announcement.

"Knock, knock."

It was her voice, calling from the pier, and he jolted, almost dropping the wineglasses he'd gotten out. "I'm below," he called.

He heard her footsteps as she crossed the deck and a moment later she was descending the stairs to the interior of the boat.

"Welcome," he said, leaning in to kiss her, lingering over the greeting until she tore her mouth away and laughed.

"I need to breathe!"

She was even more beautiful tonight than usual, her tanned skin glowing against the warmth of a pale aqua twinset that made her eyes look enormous and mysterious.

He took the basket she carried, sniffing appreciatively as the mouth-watering scent of apple cobbler permeated the air. "Wow. Can we eat this first?"

"No way." She eyed the wineglasses as he set the basket on the counter behind him. "We're going to do things in order."

Could there be a better opening? He hadn't really considered *when* he was going to tell her about Amalie, but sooner was definitely better, especially where his rolling stomach was concerned.

"Uh, Celia, why don't we sit down over here?" He heard the strain in his tone and imagined she could, too.

Her eyebrows rose. "This sound serious. Shall we have some of that wine first?"

"Sure." He slipped out his pocketknife and slit the foil, then deftly used the attached corkscrew to pull out the stopper. She held up two glasses and he filled them about halfway, then set the bottle back in the ice bucket. Taking her hand, he led her over to the couch in the entertainment area and seated her, then lowered himself beside her.

"Now what?" she asked, and he realized he'd been sitting there silently. Duh.

"I, uh, want to talk to you about something important."

"So I gather." Her eyes sparkled. "Feel free to start anytime."

He took a deep breath. Held it. Exhaled explosively. "This isn't easy to say."

Her eyes grew wary. "You're leaving." Before he could react to the assumption, she stood abruptly, setting her wineglass down with a sharp clink on the coffee table. She walked rapidly around the table and turned to face him, her mouth a determined line. Then she took a deep breath of her own. "I knew you'd go sooner or later. It's just that…" She tried to smile but her lips quivered and she pressed them tightly together for a moment. "I was getting kind of used to having you around."

His heart felt as though someone had slammed into it with a bulldozer and ground it into the dirt. He stood, walking around the table to her side and taking her elbows in his palms. "That wasn't what I wanted to say. I don't want to leave you." He swallowed. "I want to marry you."

Her mouth fell open and her eyes widened as she lifted her head and found his gaze. "You…what?"

She sounded so completely dumbfounded that he found himself feeling defensive. "I want to marry you," he repeated. "I wanted to marry you thirteen years ago and now that we've finally found each other again, I want that more than ever."

She didn't speak, only ducked her head as she stood there twisting her fingers together.

"Celia," he said to the top of her head, feeling desperate. "What are you thinking?" He lightly ran his hands up and down her arms from shoulder to elbow, as if that small contact could divine her mental state.

She smiled a little then and her eyes shone with the beginnings of tears as she met his gaze again. "We've been apart longer than we were together. Are you sure this is what you want?"

"I came looking for you, didn't I?" He took her in his arms, tenderness sweeping through him. "I love you. We were both too young the first time, or we never would have let anything separate us. But it did, and much as I regret it, I can't change that, can't get back all those wasted years. All I can do now is look forward."

"Oh, Reese," she said, "I love you, too." She laid her head on his shoulder. "Yes, I'll marry you."

Euphoria, relief, exultation swept through him like a flash flood and he suddenly felt like a superhero. He tilted her face up to his and covered her lips, kissing her with hot, deep possession and need, telling her without words what her acceptance meant to him.

But as he reluctantly ended the kiss and lifted his head, he realized what he'd just done. And more importantly, what he *hadn't* done. Cold dread slipped in, erasing the high of a moment before. But she'd just told him she still loved him. *She loved him!* Suddenly the prospect of explaining his child to her didn't seem nearly as daunting as it had a few moments before.

"Come sit down." He tugged her back to the

couch, cuddling her against his chest. "I'm getting ahead of myself."

"Where do you want to live?" she asked. "Here or Florida? Or somewhere else altogether? I wouldn't mind moving."

He cleared his throat. "I still have something to tell you before we start discussing that." When she stopped and looked at him expectantly, he marshaled his courage and cradled both her hands again, running his thumbs gently over her knuckles. "It won't just be the two of us," he told her. "I have a daughter."

Her eyes were wide, trusting, happiness shining from them with a love so strong he felt humbled. Then, as his words penetrated, the light went out.

In the merest instant, in the tiny space between one second and the next, something in her closed down so completely he could practically hear a metal door clanging shut. Her smile faded slowly until all that was left of it was a wounded expression that would haunt him until the day he died.

"You...have a child?" It was a whisper.

He nodded, holding on to her hands when she would have pulled them free. "Her name is Amalie and she's six years old. She's adopted," he said, the words falling all over each other as he tried to make her see. "I was her guardian. Her parents were the friends I told you died in the hurricane, remember? I didn't have a choice, Celia. I—"

She yanked her hands from his grip and stood, bolting around the table again. Her face was white and her eyes burned with pain. She tried to speak, choked on it and shook her head fiercely, then spoke again in a tone that was barely audible. "I told you how I felt. Right from the beginning, you knew I didn't want more children.... I told you," she repeated, her voice breaking. "I can't—"

"Can't or won't?" he demanded, fear making his voice harsh as he saw refusal on her face. "I'd like to have a child of our own someday, but I was prepared to forget about that. Amalie is—"

"I can't go through that again," she broke in. "Do you know how much it's taken for me to deal with loving you and knowing I could lose you, too?"

"You can't spend the rest of your life in a cave just because something bad might happen. What about all the wonderful times you're missing?"

"Something bad *might* happen." Tears began to roll down her cheeks and there was a torment in her eyes that made him feel as if someone were striking *him* with a whip, so sharp was the pain that radiated from her. "You don't know what it's like to lose someone you love."

"Yes. I do." He was pleading now, begging for his life. For *their* lives. "Not a child, and not in the same way you've experienced loss, but I lost thirteen years with all the people I loved most in the world."

But he might as well not have spoken.

"No," she said, backing away from him.

"Celia—" He read her intentions in her eyes and stood, and that motion was enough.

"I can't!" she said brokenly as she wheeled and bolted for the hatch. "It's not fair of you to ask me to do that."

As the sound of her ragged breathing faded, it was briefly echoed by her footfalls as she ran across the deck and up the pier.

"Celia, wait!"

But in a moment the sound of her footfalls disappeared altogether, leaving a dark, empty void into which he could feel the rest of his life sliding mercilessly. Alone…alone…alone…

"Dammit!" In a fit of rage he snatched up one of the half-full wineglasses and heaved it at the cabin wall, where it smashed with a shocking sound, spraying glass and golden liquid everywhere.

He was suddenly furious. Not only with her, but with himself. What had made him think that biology would play any role in how much Celia loved a child? She had one of the biggest hearts of anyone he'd ever met, and he realized that if she let Amalie behind those walls she'd worked so hard to erect, she would love her with every fiber of her being, as much as she would any child born of her body.

He slumped into one of the captain's chairs, his head in his hands. Despair spread steadily, invading every cell.

Oh, God, he hurt. He physically ached. He'd lost her once and forevermore had felt as if something inside him had died. And it wasn't until he'd returned and found her that his world had once again made sense.

Without her, it would never be right again. Without her… How could he start again without her?

Defeat weighed him down, sucked him under. There was no point in being here one more second, he realized. His life was what it was, and he couldn't change the way Celia felt simply because it was what he wanted.

He might as well go back to Florida. Tonight. Regardless of the emptiness that threatened to swallow him, he had a child to raise.

* * *

I can't do it. I can't do it. I can't do it.

The sentence became a litany of self-justification.

I can't do it. I can't do it. I can't do it.

"Well, I *can't!*" she said aloud as she rushed up the rise toward her cozy little house. Her mind was frozen, the only coherent thought was the denial that played over and over. She'd survived once before, when her world had been shattered, and she couldn't do it again.

He had a child. *A child!* How could he have kept a secret of that magnitude from her? Shock and fear began to recede, and anger slipped into the empty spaces. A child.

Granted, it wasn't his. And in some ridiculous way it was important to her that he hadn't fathered a child. Which, she conceded, was extremely hypocritical of her. She'd married and started a family of her own. She'd done her best to forget all about Reese Barone, and she'd been succeeding.

But he hadn't forgotten her. He'd come looking.

She knew she never would have done the same. She might have thought of him with regretful longing from time to time for the rest of her life, but she never would have had the courage to go looking for him, in hopes that after thirteen years there might still be something between them.

And you'd have missed the chance for love. You don't deserve him anyway.

That stung. Her heart thudded dully within her chest, and she put a hand over it. How much should one person be asked to handle in one lifetime? What if she married Reese and grew to love his daughter and then something happened to the child?

But you told Reese you'd marry him. What if something happened to him?

The thought was so awful she stopped walking altogether. Something could happen to Reese. No one knew it better than she. And yet, she'd said yes to his marriage proposal without giving her fears a single thought.

It was a shock to realize that sometime over the past week, the fear that had dogged her life since the day she'd gotten the news about her husband and son had receded. Yes, she still worried, but it wasn't a crippling emotion anymore. She'd been fully prepared to say yes to a life with Reese, knowing full well that there were no guarantees.

So why would it be any different with a child?

It just *was,* though she had to think about why that was so. Leo had died so young. Her biggest source of sorrow and regret was for all that he'd missed. He'd never even really had a chance to experience life before his had been taken. And she hated that, hated thinking about all the things he should have had time to try and hadn't, all because she'd let him go out on the boat with Milo that day.

And that led to the real crux of the matter. It had been her fault. *Her fault.* She was his mommy; he looked to her to protect him from anything bad, and she'd failed him.

The thought of being the anchor in another child's life terrified her. She just wasn't up to the task. She'd already failed once.

Confronting her deepest insecurity was a blinding source of light in the dark corner of her heart where she'd been nursing her fear and anger and sorrow.

I did my best, she reminded herself. *I did my best. It was not my fault.*

She repeated the words aloud—and suddenly, though she'd said the same things to herself before, this time she felt them sink into her consciousness, settle into the truths that defined her life. *I had no way of knowing there could be any danger that day.*

And she hadn't. She'd had no mystical premonition, no uneasy feeling. No way to know.

It wasn't my fault.

A ten-ton weight lifted from her shoulders. No, off her spirit. Her husband's and son's deaths had been a terrible accident, one for which she couldn't have prepared, couldn't have been responsible. And it was long past time to forgive herself, to absolve herself of blame and to let go.

Suddenly she knew without a doubt that if she hid herself away from love and life and a second chance, she'd regret it for the rest of her days. *Second? Try third.* She'd been so very lucky. Reese had been the first to teach her what love was. What she'd shared with Milo wasn't the earth-shattering, heart-swelling emotion she'd known with Reese, but it had been love. Sweet, steady and utterly comfortable. But Milo was gone and Reese had come back.

After thirteen long years he'd come back. And she'd been incredibly fortunate that the bone-deep feelings they'd known in their youth had been far, far more than raging hormones. They'd been in love and still were. A true, solid love built on that early foundation.

And she would have to be an utter fool to throw that away.

Without another thought, she turned back to the marina.

It took her about ten minutes, undoubtedly the longest of her life, to walk back. As she walked, she worked out the wording of her apology to Reese.

But when she began to walk down the pier, she got the shock of her life. The *Amalie* wasn't in her slip. Her chest grew tight, her throat felt as if someone had grabbed her and was squeezing her windpipe shut.

Where had he gone? He couldn't have left so quickly, could he?

Of course he could have. *He didn't think there was anything here to stay for, remember?*

She swallowed painfully, desolation sweeping through her. She was the one who'd rejected him. What if he never forgave her?

You're doing it again. And it had to stop. She'd spent the last few terrible years beating herself over the head and she was not going to do it anymore.

This time she wasn't going to give up. Reese loved her. He loved her enough to seek her out and to overcome her resistance. He'd made her see how extraordinary their feelings for each other were.

Now it was her turn. He'd come north to find her. She could go south and do the same thing. She had an apology to make and she intended to do it even if she had to catch a flight to Florida to deliver it. Whether or not he forgave her was beside the point. Well, okay, no it wasn't. But she had no control over that. All she could do was attempt to soothe the hurt she'd inflicted with her self-centered attitude and pray that his heart really was as big as she thought it was.

Automatically she scanned the water as she thought about what to do next. If he had left, had already gotten out onto the open ocean and up to cruising speed, she had no hope of catching up with him. The *Amalie* was one of the newest yachts on the market, with an engine to match her sleek lines.

Just as she was about to turn and walk back home again, a movement on the water caught her eye. It looked like a yacht. It looked like Reese's! She nearly cried out with happiness until she realized that what she was seeing was the stern as the boat headed away from the marina.

Then another light winked on, some distance beyond the *Amalie*. The boat appeared to be all black, barely visible against the dark sea.

And she knew, with a sickening certainty that she didn't even question, that on that boat were the people responsible for her family's deaths.

"Reese!" She screamed it even though he couldn't hear her as she ran for the shack and grabbed the keys to the nearest launch.

As she raced out the pier, a man loomed beside her, heavy footsteps pounding. "Celia," he said. "Where are you going?"

It was Ernesto Tiello, and she was briefly amazed that a man of his bulk and seeming sloth could run at all. "Reese is out there," she tossed over her shoulder, "and there's another boat that I'm certain are the drug runners everyone's been talking about are in."

They had reached the launch. "Wait," said Tiello. "I've already called for law enforcement."

"You saw them, too?"

He nodded. "We should stay here and let them handle it."

"And take a chance on those murderers getting away?" She shook her head. "No."

His face darkened. "Then take me with you."

"No," she said again as her fingers worked at the lines. "It could be dangerous."

But he was already leaping aboard the aft deck, and when he held out his palm, she saw a badge in it. "FBI," he said. "I've been after these guys since before they killed your husband and your little boy." He paused. "Claudette Mason was an agent."

Astonished, she gaped at him for a moment, then rallied, knowing there was no time to lose. "Come on. I don't want them to hurt Reese."

Tiello pulled a heavy black handgun from the back of his waistband. "Let's go."

She ran below for her binoculars, then returned to the deck and put them to her eyes and focused.

The black boat was turning and she saw a man briefly illuminated in the light that had just snapped on. He had his arms up to his shoulders—and with a shocking sense of horror and futility she knew what it was he held although she'd never seen one before in her life.

She was looking at a rocket launcher. And it was being aimed straight at Reese's boat.

Reese was madder than he'd been in years. Madder, even, than he'd been at himself thirty minutes before when he'd handled things so badly that Celia had run from the boat.

He'd pulled anchor and headed southeast away from Harwichport and the wreck he'd made of his chance for a future with her. But he'd hardly cleared the marina pier before he noticed a barely visible silhouette against the night sea just ahead of him. No running lights. He narrowed his eyes, realizing that whatever was out there was a decent-size yacht. His pulse kicked up a notch as he realized he might have inadvertently stumbled onto Claudette Mason's killers and he made an instant decision.

A moment later he had the Coast Guard emergency response on the line. If he was mistaken, the worst that could happen was that he embarrassed himself and had to apologize to some innocent person. If he wasn't, it was just possible that the men Celia had been hunting so diligently were less than a mile away from him.

Celia. God, it hurt even to think her name. He shook himself, refusing to allow himself to linger on the ugly scene they'd just played out.

He got out his binoculars while he talked to the dispatcher, but there was little to be seen even with the strong magnification. The boat was dark in color all over and if there was anyone about, he couldn't see them.

Then, as nicely as if he'd asked, a light came on. Three people, clearly visible with the binoculars, stood on deck. One was a large man whom he'd never seen before. The other two... His stomach flipped over and shock rushed through him, making his scalp tingle. There was a man as well as a woman standing on deck with the large man. The second man was trim and small and neat. Neil Brevery. One of the people to whom Celia rented a slip.

Claudette had worked for Brevery; how coincidental was that? His suspicions grew as he continued to survey the boat. And then he trained his binoculars on Brevery's companion and the breath went out of his lungs.

Rage kindled and began to build. The third person

on the deck of the other boat was Celia's assistant, Angie. God, had she been working with a killer?

Grimly he went below and unlocked the rifle he kept in a safe place in his stateroom. The Coast Guard had said they had gotten one call and were on their way, but he was taking no chances. The other boat wasn't going anywhere.

Moving back on deck, he gunned his engine and pushed the yacht up to speed, heading directly for the other yacht, the rifle under his arm, barrel down. He grabbed the binoculars again for a closer view.

Brevery and Angie looked as if they were arguing. They both were at the rail, peering in his direction as the boat steadily turned around.

Could it be true? Could that harmless-looking young woman be responsible for Claudette's murder? For the deaths of Celia's family?

It was hard to fathom. Maybe he'd leaped way off base in search of an answer, but he'd rather be wrong than let them get away.

Swinging the binoculars to starboard, he focused on the third man. The guy was large, unfamiliar, but the thing he lifted to his shoulder, which looked like a length of plumbing pipe from this distance, raised the hair on the back of Reese's neck.

As the man aimed the weapon—and he knew that was exactly what it was—straight at the *Amalie,* survival instincts took over and Reese dove over the rail as far as he could from the boat.

Nine

"**N**oooooo!"

Celia screamed as she saw a flash and watched a trail of fire fly straight at Reese's boat. A second later she took a deep gasp of relief as the rocket sailed over the boat and splashed harmlessly into the sea.

But then, as her uncomprehending gaze swung back to the dark boat, a second shot flared. It hung in the air, speeding straight for Reese's yacht, and she screamed again, helplessly, as the *Amalie* blew apart in a roiling cloud of smoke and flame.

Ernesto Tiello cursed vividly, standing beside her at the wheel. Then he pointed at the sky. "Look," he shouted.

A helicopter had appeared, winging low over the water, and from the same direction Celia could see the powerful searchlights of three launches speeding toward the black boat, which was attempting to turn and put on speed. Her heart was a leaden weight in her chest and she registered the drama distantly, but her attention was fixed on the dusky blotch of smoke that still marked the site of the explosion. She kept a steady course for the spot where Reese's boat had gone down, although the chase was moving off in another direction.

Please, please, please. Please let him be there.

As they approached, bits of debris began to appear, shattered lengths of timber, rags, buckets and empty life preservers, a deck chair half-submerged. Despair swamped her.

Dear Lord, please. Not again.

But hope waned as they circled the area. There was no sign of a body. No sizable pieces of debris bigger than a four-foot length of wood. The second assault must have been a direct hit, she realized, sinking the yacht within moments. By the time the worst of the obscuring smoke had cleared, the *Amalie* was no more.

Panic fluttered behind her breastbone and she beat it back fiercely as she continued to scan the water. Reese was still alive. He had to be. *He had to be.*

A boat approached, a white Coast Guard launch, and she listened with half an ear as Ernesto talked with them. The other boat had been apprehended, the three people aboard taken into custody. She turned briefly when she heard that Mr. Brevery was the brains of the business, and that Angie Dunstan had been his eyes and ears locally.

She was stunned. "Angie…?" and the two men nodded.

Blindly she turned back around to the sea. Angie. Celia still thought of her as a girl even though she knew Angie was twenty-two now. Milo had hired the young woman fresh out of high school. She'd been pleasant, efficient—and probably responsible for his death, Celia realized suddenly.

Then a movement on the water caught her eye.

Hope surged.

"Reese!" It was a hoarse scream and both Tiello and the men aboard the Coast Guard cutter whipped around to stare at her. She barely noticed, already gunning the engine as she marked the feeble lift of a hand in the far-off swells.

"Hang on, Reese," she called again and again as they neared him. Ernesto had climbed over the ladder and lowered his bulky body into the sea; she maneuvered the launch as close as she dared, while Tiello dragged Reese aboard the boat.

He had a deep gash across his forehead and one arm hung at an odd angle as they lay him down and covered him with blankets. Tiello got on the radio, requesting air transport to a medical facility, while Celia took the thermal blankets the Coast Guard had tossed aboard and tenderly tucked them around Reese. Hypothermia was a real danger in the cold autumn waters of the North Atlantic and the relief she'd felt dissipated quickly as she took in the pallor of his face and his blue lips.

"Shh," she said when he moved restlessly. "Don't try to talk. We're going to get you to a hospital."

He lifted his good hand and indicated the sea, and she realized he wanted to know what had happened. "They sank your boat," she began, but he shook his head.

"I know," he said. "Wh-wh…where…?"

"They're in custody." She smiled down at him.

"Coming after you was their downfall. It gave the Coast Guard and the FBI time to get to them."

"An-An-An—"

She nodded, her smile fading. "Angie. I know." She shook her head, wondering at the amorality that had allowed the young woman to work side by side with the widow and mother of the innocent people she'd had a hand in killing.

Reese's hand lifted, stroked down her cheekbone, and she focused on him again. "You're freezing. We've got to get you to a hospital."

"T-talk." It was a demand, and she smiled, letting the love she felt for him shine in her eyes as she dropped her head and brushed a kiss over his chilly lips.

"We'll talk later. Everything's going to be fine."

Everything's going to be fine.

He clung to the words, and to the memory of her kiss, while he was airlifted to the nearest hospital and his injuries were treated.

His left arm was fractured, he needed stitches to close gashes on his forehead and his back, and he felt bruised all over, as if he'd been beaten with a giant pipe over every inch of his body. They told him he had a concussion, which might explain the fuzzy vision and the way his mind kept losing track of what he'd been thinking about.

Everything's going to be fine.

What had she meant? Had it simply been reassurance for an injured man? Surely she wouldn't have kissed him if that were the case. And what had she been doing out on the water anyway?

"Mr. Barone?" The emergency room doctor came

in. "I'd like to admit you overnight for observation. Given your—"

"No," said Reese.

"Yes." The voice was feminine, familiar, and his heart began to beat faster. When he turned his head to look, Celia stood in the doorway. Actually, to his concussed eyes, there appeared to be two of her standing there. "He'll stay," she told the doctor.

"Only if you stay with me," he told her.

She smiled and he felt something tight and fearful inside his chest ease for the first time since she'd rushed off his boat. "You've got a deal," she said.

They took him to a private room on an upper floor. Celia walked beside the gurney on which he lay and held his hand, and he allowed himself the smallest glimmer of hope.

"I called Nick."

"Why?" He was a little startled. It never would have occurred to him to contact his brother.

"It's going to make the papers, Reese," she said patiently. "You wouldn't want your family to find out from a newspaper article that you were almost killed."

He was silent for a minute. "You're right. Thank you." Then a thought struck him. "If I give you the number, would you...would you call down to Florida for me?"

"Yes." Her voice sounded noncommittal, and renewed fear dampened his budding hope.

Once he was settled and all the hospital personnel had come and gone, there was silence in the small room. Celia sat in a reclining chair beside the bed. She'd pulled it around so she could face him, and her hand was clasped in his atop the sheet.

"Reese," she said.

"Hmm?" His head hurt. Everything hurt. Even his eyes hurt when he moved them to look at her. And he was afraid, frankly. Afraid to talk, in case he was wrong and she didn't still—

"I love you."

Suddenly the aches and pains of a moment before seemed far less debilitating. "I love you, too. Wanna come up here and show me?"

She laughed. "Not a chance, buddy."

There was another silence and he was sorry he'd been flippant. This was too important for stupid jokes. He couldn't stand it. "Celia—"

"Shh. We'll talk later." She lifted his hand and brushed a kiss across the knuckles, then looked him dead in the eye. "I'm not going anywhere ever again."

He'd slept at last, waking only when the nurses checked his pupils periodically, and coming to when the breakfast tray arrived in the morning.

Celia had stayed through the night, leaving only to run to her home and bring him a set of clean clothes. It was a good thing he'd left a few at her house, she thought, remembering his beautiful boat sadly. Then she shook herself. The boat could be replaced. Reese couldn't, and she was so very thankful he was safe.

When she returned, he'd already eaten and bathed and was scanning the morning paper, awkwardly turning the outsize pages with his good hand. The other was in a temporary cast, which would be replaced when the swelling subsided, and he wore it in a sling across his chest.

"Hi," he said softly as she entered the room.

"Hi." She knew it was ridiculous to be nervous, but she had to stop herself from twisting her fingers together.

"Come sit down." Reese patted the edge of the bed.

Carefully she went to him and seated herself at his side. "How do you feel this morning?"

He smiled. "Like one of those cartoon animals that gets mashed flat by a boulder or a truck."

She had to laugh, but the memory of the *Amalie* disintegrating into a shocking ball of flame superceded the amusement, and, to her dismay, she suddenly found herself fighting tears.

"Hey." Reese put his arm around her and gently pulled her against his shoulder, stroking her back. "It's okay."

"I thought you were dead." She kept her face pressed into his neck and curled against his side, careful not to jostle the damaged arm between them.

"Shh." She felt him kiss her temple. "I thought I was dead, too, when I saw that rocket launcher aimed my way. It seemed to take forever before the thing actually blew up my boat."

"He fired two," she recalled. "The first one missed."

"That explains it. I dove over the side and swam away from the boat as fast as I could. The missed shot probably saved my life." He shook his head slightly. "Even so, the blast rolled me through the water like a damned doll. I don't remember what happened after that."

"You must have been hit by debris. You've got a couple of nasty cuts in addition to that arm."

"I know." She felt him smile and his voice was

rueful. "I remembered when I started moving around this morning. Man, did they ever sting." He pulled her slightly away from him and looked down into her eyes. "Can we talk now?"

She nodded. "I'm sorry, Reese. I've spent the past couple of years trying to protect myself from getting hurt ever again. After I left last night, I realized that life makes no guarantees. I'd already let you back into my heart, and if anything happens to you—" Her voice wavered.

"Celia—"

She held up her hand. "Let me get this out." She took a deep breath. "I would be honored to marry you and be a mother to Amalie. If you still want me," she added in a small voice.

"If I still want you?" His voice was hushed. "Woman, I've wanted you forever. I love you, Celia." He touched his lips to hers. "I was wrong not to tell you I had a kid right up front. But I knew how much it would hurt you, and I—I was afraid. Afraid you might not give me a second chance if you knew I came with a sidekick."

She laid her head on his shoulder and sighed. "Your instincts probably were right. I might not have."

Reese turned his head and sought her lips again, capturing her in a sweet, hot exchange that left her breathless. "As soon as that doctor checks me over, I'm getting out of here and we're going to get married."

She smiled. "I don't think we can just go get married today."

"We can if we fly to Vegas." His voice sounded utterly serious, and her heart turned over.

"You've got me there. But—" She shook her head. "I'm not letting you go anywhere until the doctor gives you the go-ahead."

He had already opened his mouth to respond when the door swished open. "All right, Doc," he said. "It's about time…" His voice trailed away.

Celia had turned and tried to put some space between them, but Reese held her in place as an older man and woman walked into the room. She was afraid to hurt him by pushing against his chest, so she let him keep her there at his side.

The man wasn't as tall as Reese but she knew in a heartbeat who he was. Reese's father still had thick dark hair, though silver shone at his temples, and she had a sudden vivid image of what Reese would look like in thirty years.

The woman with him was gorgeous, her figure stunning, her hair a vibrant red. There were a few threads of silver in it, as well, or Celia never would have believed that this woman could be old enough to be Reese's mother.

Mrs. Barone had tears in her eyes. "Reese," she said, coming to the side of the bed. "Nick called us. I know we might not be welcome but…we wanted to see for ourselves that you're all right." She put out a hand, then tugged it back and held it against her waist. To Celia, it appeared that she desperately wanted to hug Reese, but was unsure of her reception.

"Thank you for coming. As you can see, I'm a little banged up but essentially okay." Reese's voice was neutral. A part of her wanted to kick him, but she recognized the insecurity hiding beneath his calm surface. He was afraid to be rejected again.

"Reese." His father cleared his throat, his eyes

steady as they rested on his son's. "I owe you an apology for leaping to the wrong conclusion all those years ago. I'm sorry I left it so long. When you didn't come home... I thought that you no longer wanted to be in contact with us and I couldn't blame you."

Reese was silent for a moment. The tension in the room was so thick, Celia understood for the first time what people meant when they said they could cut it with a knife. She had a ridiculous urge to get the small pocketknife from her purse and try it.

Finally, Reese said, "Thank you. I apologize, too, for losing my temper and staying away so long." He turned then and took her hand. "Mother, Dad, this is Celia Papaleo." Although there wasn't exactly a note of challenge in his voice, she recognized that he was using her as a test.

Mrs. Barone immediately offered an outstretched hand to Celia across the bed. "It's so nice to meet you at last, Celia. Please call us Carlo and Moira." She gave the younger woman a warm, genuine smile. "Reese spoke of you often when he was younger. I know you're very special to him."

"As are you." Celia went with instinct and leaned forward, embracing Moira Barone in a warm hug. "Thank you."

"It is truly a pleasure, Celia," Carlo Barone said. He came around the end of the bed to where she sat and kissed her formally on each cheek in a courtly manner.

She nodded, smiling at him as he stepped back.

"Celia has just agreed to marry me." The announcement fell into the momentary silence.

His mother made a small sound of delight. "Congratulations!"

"Welcome to the family," Carlo said to Celia. "Everyone is anxious to see Reese again. They'll all be thrilled to hear this news."

"Have you set a date?" asked Moira.

"Um, no," Celia said. "We're very newly engaged."

"She just said yes before you walked in the door," Reese said, grinning.

"So that's what we interrupted," Carlo said to his wife. "See, I told you we should have knocked!"

"We're not planning on a long engagement." Reese dragged the conversation back to the earlier topic. "In fact, if I have my way, we'll be husband and wife right away." He paused, giving his parents a conspiratorial grin. "How would you like to fly to Vegas and witness our wedding?"

"We'd love to," his mother answered.

"He means today," Celia informed them. She turned to Reese. "You really need to rest—"

"I really need to marry you. Today." He caught her hand and pressed a kiss to her knuckles. "We've waited too long as it is."

Carlo Barone was laughing. "You might as well stop arguing, Celia. Nobody wins an argument with a Barone man."

"Ha." Moira winked at Celia. "You just let him keep on thinking that for the next fifty years and you'll do just fine together."

Reese tugged on her hand, pulling her down to the edge of the bed. When she acceded, he immediately drew her to him for a kiss, and as she thought of how close she'd come to losing him, she sank against him with a quiet sigh. He'd told her he was born to be wild, but she'd had enough wild to last her a lifetime already.

A lifetime. She kissed him back fervently, forgetting all about their audience. She knew better than most how fragile happiness could be. If he wanted to get married today, she'd do it.

And then she wanted to meet his daughter—*their* daughter—and start living the rest of their lives together.

*   *   *   *   *

DYNASTIES: THE BARONES

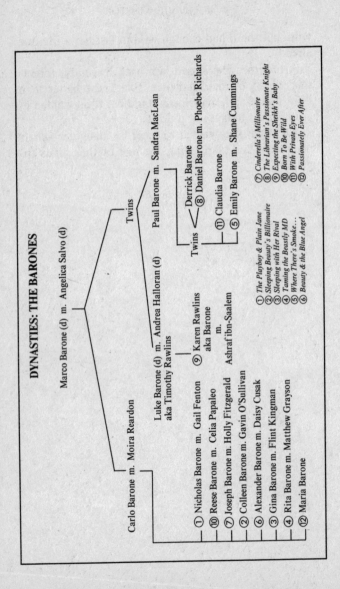

Marco Barone (d) m. Angelica Salvo (d)

Carlo Barone m. Moira Reardon

Luke Barone (d) m. Andrea Halloran (d)
aka Timothy Rawlins

⑨ Karen Rawlins
aka Barone
m.
Ashraf ibn-Saalem

Twins

Paul Barone m. Sandra MacLean

Derrick Barone
⑧ Daniel Barone m. Phoebe Richards

Twins

⑪ Claudia Barone

⑤ Emily Barone m. Shane Cummings

① Nicholas Barone m. Gail Fenton
⑩ Reese Barone m. Celia Papaleo
⑦ Joseph Barone m. Holly Fitzgerald
② Colleen Barone m. Gavin O'Sullivan
⑥ Alexander Barone m. Daisy Cusak
③ Gina Barone m. Flint Kingman
④ Rita Barone m. Matthew Grayson
⑫ Maria Barone

① The Playboy & Plain Jane
② Sleeping Beauty's Billionaire
③ Sleeping with Her Rival
④ Taming the Beastly MD
⑤ Where There's Smoke...
⑥ Beauty & the Blue Angel

⑦ Cinderella's Millionaire
⑧ The Librarian's Passionate Knight
⑨ Expecting the Sheikh's Baby
⑩ Born To Be Wild
⑪ With Private Eyes
⑫ Passionately Ever After

DYNASTIES: THE BARONES
continues...

Turn the page for a bonus look at what's in store for you in the next Barones book— only from Silhouette Desire!

WITH PRIVATE EYES
by Eileen Wilks
November 2003
(#1543)

One

Uncle Miles had always told him his sense of humor would get him hung one of these days, Ethan reflected. Maybe today was the day.

"I'd like to start as soon as possible." The blonde sitting on the other side of his desk gave him a bright smile. "This is going to make a terrific article."

Maybe it was his curiosity that would get him in trouble this time. As much as it tickled his sense of the absurd for Claudia Barone to present herself in his office posing as a reporter, he wouldn't have let her run through her spiel if he hadn't wanted to know what she was up to. "I haven't agreed yet," he pointed out.

"Oh, well." She said that tolerantly and crossed her legs, sliding one long, silky thigh over the other. "How can I persuade you?"

Then again, those legs might be the real culprit.

The moment she'd appeared in his doorway in her lipstick-red suit he'd wanted to get her into the visitor's chair in front of his desk. He'd wanted to find out how much that one-inch-too-short hiked up.

They were world-class legs, he thought regretfully. And she knew it. She'd crossed and uncrossed them four times since she sat down. "I don't imagine you can."

Not a whit discouraged, she launched into a repetition of her asinine story, her hands flying enthusiastically. It was an intriguing contrast, he thought. Her posture was very proper—shoulders squared, spine straight—and she certainly didn't raise her voice. But her gestures were as loud as the color of her suit.

Even on ten minutes' acquaintance, he could tell Claudia Barone was crammed with contradictions. She looked like the prototype for a tall, cool sip of blond elegance. She was pale and slim—*too skinny,* he told himself—with blue eyes and classic features marred by a nose too assertive for its setting. Her honey-colored hair was pulled back in a kind of roll at the back, very sleek and polished. Her suit was conservative, too, if you ignored where the hemline hit.

And the color. Which was echoed in the siren-red gloss she'd sleeked over a cute little rosebud mouth.

Her story might be crazy, but her voice was worth listening to, even if it did tug at memories he'd prefer stayed safely buried...

*   *   *   *   *

From
Katherine Garbera

CINDERELLA'S CHRISTMAS AFFAIR

Silhouette Desire #1546

With the help of a matchmaking
angel in training, two ugly-ducklings-
turned-swans experience passion and
love…and a little holiday magic.

You're on his hit list.

*Available November 2003
at your favorite retail outlet.*

✂ **Your opinion is important to us!** Please take a few moments to share your thoughts with us about your experiences with Harlequin and Silhouette books. Your comments will be very useful in ensuring that we deliver books you love to read. *Please take a few minutes to complete the questionnaire, then send it to us at the address below.*

Send your completed questionnaires to:
Harlequin/Silhouette Reader Survey, P.O. Box 9046, Buffalo, NY 14269-9046

1. As you may know, there are many different lines under the Harlequin and Silhouette brands. Each of the lines is listed below. Please check the box that most represents your reading habit for each line.

Line	Currently read this line	Do not read this line	Not sure if I read this line
Harlequin American Romance	❏	❏	❏
Harlequin Duets	❏	❏	❏
Harlequin Romance	❏	❏	❏
Harlequin Historicals	❏	❏	❏
Harlequin Superromance	❏	❏	❏
Harlequin Intrigue	❏	❏	❏
Harlequin Presents	❏	❏	❏
Harlequin Temptation	❏	❏	❏
Harlequin Blaze	❏	❏	❏
Silhouette Special Edition	❏	❏	❏
Silhouette Romance	❏	❏	❏
Silhouette Intimate Moments	❏	❏	❏
Silhouette Desire	❏	❏	❏

2. Which of the following best describes why you bought *this book*? One answer only, please.

the picture on the cover	❏	the title	❏
the author	❏	the line is one I read often	❏
part of a miniseries	❏	saw an ad in another book	❏
saw an ad in a magazine/newsletter	❏	a friend told me about it	❏
I borrowed/was given this book	❏	other: _____	❏

3. Where did you buy *this book*? One answer only, please.

at Barnes & Noble	❏	at a grocery store	❏
at Waldenbooks	❏	at a drugstore	❏
at Borders	❏	on eHarlequin.com Web site	❏
at another bookstore	❏	from another Web site	❏
at Wal-Mart	❏	Harlequin/Silhouette Reader	❏
at Target	❏	Service/through the mail	
at Kmart	❏	used books from anywhere	❏
at another department store or mass merchandiser	❏	I borrowed/was given this book	❏

4. On average, how many Harlequin and Silhouette books do you buy at one time?

I buy _____ books at one time	❏
I rarely buy a book	❏

MRQ403SD-1A

5. How many times per month do you shop for any *Harlequin and/or Silhouette* books?
   One answer only, please.

1 or more times a week	❏	a few times per year	❏
1 to 3 times per month	❏	less often than once a year	❏
1 to 2 times every 3 months	❏	never	❏

6. When you think of your ideal heroine, which *one* statement describes her the best?
   One answer only, please.

She's a woman who is strong-willed	❏	She's a desirable woman	❏
She's a woman who is needed by others	❏	She's a powerful woman	❏
She's a woman who is taken care of	❏	She's a passionate woman	❏
She's an adventurous woman	❏	She's a sensitive woman	❏

7. The following statements describe types or genres of books that you may be
   interested in reading. Pick *up to 2 types* of books that you are most interested in.

I like to read about truly romantic relationships	❏
I like to read stories that are sexy romances	❏
I like to read romantic comedies	❏
I like to read a romantic mystery/suspense	❏
I like to read about romantic adventures	❏
I like to read romance stories that involve family	❏
I like to read about a romance in times or places that I have never seen	❏
Other: _____	❏

*The following questions help us to group your answers with those readers who are
similar to you. Your answers will remain confidential.*

8. Please record your year of birth below.
   19 ____

9. What is your marital status?
   single ❏   married ❏   common-law ❏   widowed ❏
   divorced/separated ❏

10. Do you have children 18 years of age or younger currently living at home?
    yes ❏   no ❏

11. Which of the following best describes your employment status?
    employed full-time or part-time ❏   homemaker ❏   student ❏
    retired ❏   unemployed ❏

12. Do you have access to the Internet from either home or work?
    yes ❏   no ❏

13. Have you ever visited eHarlequin.com?
    yes ❏   no ❏

14. What state do you live in?

    _____

15. Are you a member of Harlequin/Silhouette Reader Service?
    yes ❏   Account #_____   no ❏   MRQ403SD-1B

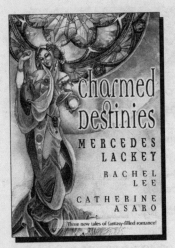

TEXAS
CATTLEMAN'S CLUB:
The Stolen Baby

A powerful miniseries featuring
six wealthy Texas bachelors—
all members of the state's most
prestigious club—who set out
to unravel the mystery surrounding
one tiny baby...and discover true love
in the process!

The newest installment launches with

ENTANGLED WITH A TEXAN
by Sara Orwig
(Silhouette Desire #1547)

Meet David Sorrenson—ex-military
and notorious ladies' man. He'd hired
Marissa Wilder to help him watch over
the little girl left in his care. But having the
sexy nanny living under the same roof
was tying this confirmed bachelor
in serious knots!

Available November 2003 at your favorite retail outlet.

COMING NEXT MONTH

#1543 WITH PRIVATE EYES—Eileen Wilks
Dynasties: The Barones
Socialite Claudia Barone *insisted* on helping investigate the attempted sabotage of her family's business. But detective Ethan Mallory had a hard head to match his hard body. He always worked on his own….he didn't need the sexy sophisticate on the case. What he *wanted*…well, that was another matter!

#1544 BABY, YOU'RE MINE—Peggy Moreland
The Tanners of Texas
In one moment, Woodrow Tanner changed Dr. Elizabeth Montgomery's life. The gruff-yet-sexy rancher had come bearing news of her estranged sister's death—and the existence of Elizabeth's baby niece. Even as Elizabeth tried to accept this startling news, she couldn't help but crave Woodrow's consoling embrace….

#1545 WILD IN THE FIELD—Jennifer Greene
The Lavender Trilogy
Like the fields of lavender growing outside her window, Camille Campbell looked sweet and delicate, but could thrive even in the harshest conditions. Divorced dad and love-wary neighbor Pete MacDougal found in Camille a kindred soul…whose body could elicit in him the most amazing feelings….

#1546 CINDERELLA'S CHRISTMAS AFFAIR—Katherine Garbera
King of Hearts
Brawny businessman Tad Randolph promised his parents he'd be married with children before Christmas—and cool-as-ice executive CJ Terrance was the perfect partner for his pretend wedding and baby-making scheme. But soon Tad realized she was more fire than ice…and found himself wishing CJ shared more than just his bed!

#1547 ENTANGLED WITH A TEXAN—Sara Orwig
Texas Cattleman's Club: The Stolen Baby
A certain sexy rancher was the stuff of fantasies for baby store clerk Marissa Wilder. So when David Sorrenson showed up needing Marissa's help, she quickly agreed to be a temporary live-in nanny for the mystery baby David was caring for. But could she convince her fantasy man to care for *her*, as well?

#1548 AWAKENING BEAUTY—Amy J. Fetzer
There was more to dowdy bookseller Lane Douglas than met the eye…and Tyler McKay was determined to find out her secrets. Resisting the magnetic millionaire was difficult for Lane, but she vowed to keep her identity under wraps…even as her heart and body threatened to betray her.